DAMAGED

SOUTH SIDE BOYS BOOK 1

ALEXIS WINTER

A NOVEL

By
Alexis Winter

I'M DAMAGED. DARK. HAUNTED.

A shell of a man with no hope for a future.
Annabelle Locke is Innocent and pure.
Is she my cure?
A bright light of hope in my cold world?
She's everything I want and everything I don't deserve.
I thought I could have a taste and walk away.
Now the shadows from my past have returned and I'll stop at nothing
to keep her safe.
Even if that means I have to lose her forever.
She can't know the secrets from my past.
She can't know the truth of who I really am.
Or what I've done.

But maybe it's too late…

ANNABELLE

S hit. Shit. Shit.

Know those days where you swear it's Thursday, but the universe is insistent on treating it like a Monday?

Welcome to my Thursday.

Normally I'm pretty good balancing trays, coffee, orders, and traffic with baristas at Perks, the café I manage in Chicago. I'm an artist—a painter, more specifically. Or at least in another life I was. Steady hands are needed to create works of beauty.

But today? Apparently, whoever is directing traffic for my life is deciding to mess with me in the worst way possible.

This morning I spilled coffee that somehow missed my apron and landed squarely on the sleeves of my white button-down blouse. My hairdryer finally bit the dust, so my auburn hair is wrapped into some sort of topknot that's not as cute as the women on Pinterest make it out to be.

But the coup de grâce? The exclamation point on an already shit-tastic day? Dropping a tray of samples on the floor when *he* walked in. Hence the trail of obscenities that I thought I said in my head, but judging by the looks I'm getting from customers, were very much verbalized.

Great. Not only am I a klutz, but I'm also a foul-mouthed klutz.

I don't even know why I'm freaking out. The customers are all regulars. They've seen their fair share of spills and broken mugs.

Okay, I do know why.

It's because of him. Mr. Dark and Dangerous.

"Girl, why are you a hot mess express today?" my best friend and coworker, Tori, asks me as she bends down to help me pick up the tray full of mini sandwiches I dropped on the floor. "This is completely not like you."

As we scramble to pick up the scattered sandwiches, I look up to see Mr. Dark and Dangerous at the counter, ordering a large black coffee.

It's always the same. I don't have to see the front of him to know what he's ordering.

Though I can't see the transaction, I can see his very firm backside that leads up to his muscled back and broad shoulders. Then there are the tattoos that travel up and down his arms. Arms that fight a daily battle to stay confined in his tight T-shirts.

I'm drooling. I know I am. He's the most gorgeous man I've ever seen in real life.

"Quit staring at Mr. Dark and Dangerous or we're going to have to get the mop for the puddle you'll leave on the floor. And with your luck today, you'll slip on your own saliva."

I shake myself out of my not-so-subtle stare and walk back behind the counter. He's leaving now, and I can't help but peek one more time at the man who has rendered me speechless since the first time he walked into Perks.

I had just started—only been here for a few weeks—when he walked in. I literally stopped all movement. I had never seen a man like him. Yes, he was hot in that bad boy kind of way, but there was something else about him.

As soon as he came to the counter and looked down at me—I'm 5'3" on a good day, so everyone looks down at me—I became enthralled.

His eyes. They were like dark chocolate but so . . . intense. That's the only word I could think of to describe them.

I could barely greet him when he came up to order. Thankfully, he ordered his large coffee, tossed $5 on the counter and nodded before turning to leave.

And that's how it is every single time. How is it that when he visits, it's the highlight as well as the worst part of my day?

"Are you ever going to talk to him?" Tori asks, bumping my hip to knock me back into reality. "Your eyes bug out every time he walks in. He must know that you like him. Just talk to him! At least ask him his name so we can stop calling him Mr. Dark and Dangerous! It's a fun nickname, but man is it a mouthful."

I laugh at my best friend, who made up the name when we realized we didn't know his. Unfortunately, we're not like Starbucks, so we don't ask for names when we take orders. Maybe we should start doing that?

I might not know his name, but I know he's the star in my fantasies every night. And that's just fine for me. Honestly, even having him *there* is too much to handle.

"Tori, you know I'm never going to talk to him. What would I say? I can barely look at the man— can you imagine me trying to talk to him?"

If she thinks I would ever have the guts to talk to him, she's out of her mind. I'm not exactly experienced when it comes to men. I've only had one serious boyfriend and that ended horribly. But it brought me to Chicago and the start of my new life. Everything happens for a reason, right?

I moved to Chicago about six months ago—a dream I've had for so long I can't remember a time I didn't want to be in this city. In those dreams, I was a famous artist living in the Windy City, with my paintings displayed in my own trendy gallery in Hyde Park. My parents would drive in for my exhibits and show nothing but pride on their faces as their only daughter was living her best life.

But life happens. Dreams change. In ways you'd never expect. I've experienced that more times than I care to admit.

Instead of a famous artist, or even a budding one, I'm the manager at Perks. It's nice. I have great co-workers, and meeting Tori was more than I could have asked for when I moved here. Where I'm petite, slender, and can be on the quiet side, she's tall, athletic, and is the life of the party.

We're a great balance. She gets me out of my comfort zone, and I rein her in. Or at least try to.

"I can help you. You know I always know what to say to guys," she says. That might sound cocky to some, but I know it's the truth. "I mean, let's at least find out his name. What about, 'Hi. I'm Annabelle. I don't know what to scream out when I use my vibrator thinking of you every night, so how about you give me something to work with?'"

I throw my towel as I laugh at my ridiculous best friend.

"You're insane. You know that will never happen."

"I just want you to be happy. And to have fun. You don't have enough of it. And I bet Mr. Dark and Dangerous could provide plenty of fun, if you know what I mean."

I shake my head and walk away. She won't give this up, and I don't have another comeback. I'm sure he would be fun. More fun than I could handle.

He's Mr. Dark and Dangerous—covered in tattoos with testosterone oozing from every pore on his hard body.

I'm a virgin from the suburbs who would have no idea how to handle a man like that.

JAXSON

"You're going to need to sign these. And here's the purchase order for the new mats, so you're going to need to review those before they're processed. Oh, and be sure to check on those new gloves and wrist wraps you purchased that aren't in yet."

No one told me running my own gym would come with so much fucking paperwork.

After I scribble my barely readable signature on the last form, I sit back and take a sip from my cup of coffee. My afternoon caffeine jolt from the place a few blocks over always does the trick.

I turn my desk chair around so I can look down at the main gym. There's a ring to the right where two kids no older than 19 are sparring. To the left is the octagon, where a class is currently being taught. And there's another section with mats on the floors and walls.

And it's all mine. I did this.

Who'd have thought that I, Jaxson Kelly, fuck-up from the South Side, convicted felon and son of a lowlife bookie, could pull something like this off?

I continue to watch the action in the gym for a few more minutes, deciding that I'm going to get in some ring time tonight, and turn back around to see Reggie, my business partner and co-owner of the gym, still standing in front of my desk.

"Dude, why are you still here? Don't tell me there are other forms to sign."

"I had one more thing to talk to you about, but wanted all the signatures first because it could piss you off and I didn't want you throwing me out."

I've known Reggie for a few years now. We did time together in prison. Me for being on a second strike and knocking some fucker out cold, who didn't know the meaning of the word *no* despite being a cop. Reggie was in for burglary. We were in the same cell block, and even though I'm not the talking type, Reggie and I became brothers. You need someone on the inside to keep your head on straight.

We came up with the idea of the gym one night during chow, and at first we played it off as a pipe dream. Then as our release days got closer, we knew we needed something when we got out, and neither of us wanted to work for someone else.

So here we are. I take care of operations; he keeps us in the black. And clean. That was the one thing we were dead set on—making sure this business was on the straight and narrow. Between the two of us, we have too many ghosts from the past, and we know we need to keep them there.

I take another sip of my coffee, waiting for Reggie to drop whatever bomb he's holding. I consider throwing the coffee at him if I don't like what he's about to say, but it's too good to waste.

"How is that coffee place? You go there a lot."

"You want to talk to me about coffee?" I know he's stalling. And so am I. I'm not telling him that even though the coffee is damn good, the scenery is much better. More specifically, the cute little redhead I could fit in my pocket.

"No. Okay. Here goes," he takes in a deep breath. "We're going to need to put one of the new classes on hold. I was taking out the trash today and noticed when I walked in the back alley that someone fucked with the outdoor camera. We might be in a better part of town than where we came from, but you know we can't *not* have security.

And honestly, it needs an upgrade. That's going to cost money, which means we can't afford to pay another instructor."

He's right. This news does piss me off.

"Cut the kickboxing classes for now, but let's try to get them on the schedule no later than three months from now."

"I was thinking of the self-defense instructor. He costs more money and—"

"No!" I bark at Reggie. He's seen my temper before, but even this is taking him by surprise. "The self-defense class stays. I don't care if I have to pay for the new fucking system out of my own pocket if that's what it'll take to keep that class going."

Reggie takes a few seconds to gather himself after my outburst. I'm not surprised this takes him by surprise. We might have done time together, and he might know more about me than just about anyone else, but he has no clue about everything I've been through. And why offering this class means so much to me.

Hell, it's half the reason I opened this place: to ensure women could protect themselves.

If I couldn't protect her, at least I could help protect others.

I don't let my mind go down that road. I'm already wound up tight and need to go a few rounds. Thinking of my baby sister won't put me in the right headspace, and I don't need to accidentally beat the shit out of another sparring partner.

"Okay. Well then, I'll fix the schedule and delay the kickboxing classes. And I'll do my best to get them back on the schedule sooner rather than later."

"Thanks, man. Sorry I blew up like that."

He shakes his head and stands up to leave. "No worries. Just didn't know you were so passionate about self-defense classes."

And he won't ever know the reason behind it. No one will. Ever.

3

ANNABELLE

I can't believe I just pulled that off. I couldn't keep the smile off my face as I finished wiping down the counters in the café.

Tonight was a big night for Perks. About a month ago, I had an idea for live music a few nights a week—just for a few hours, until we closed at 11. The owner loved it and told me to run with it. We have so many musicians in this city—some who are trying to make it big and some who just want to perform on the side—that it wasn't hard to line up acts for the next month.

We always do well during the daytime hours, but nights have always been a bit slow, and I thought this would boost the night crowd.

And boy, did it! So much so that once the night began, I didn't stop serving drinks until we turned the lights up at 11. And luckily, there were no spills, breaks, or any other type of catastrophe today.

Even though being the manager at Perks isn't exactly my dream job, it was nice to feel a sense of accomplishment. Right now I have the same feeling I used to get when I finished a painting: the satisfaction of completing a project and seeing an idea come to life. It's something many people take for granted. I used to. And I never will again.

8

Life is too short to not celebrate the little victories. We aren't promised a tomorrow.

We were a skeleton crew, just me plus Kristina, a nice girl who works a few hours a week after school. Earlier in the day, someone had called in to say they couldn't make it, and no one wanted to pick up a last-minute shift on a Friday night, so I got it. I'd rather not work on a Friday night either. But it's not like I had anything else to do other than continue my latest Netflix binge with takeout Chinese food.

The problem was that Kristina, still being 17, couldn't stay after 10 p.m. So it was just me closing up the shop.

I didn't mind though. I cranked up my music as I counted the money in the drawers and disassembled the machines for the night.

With a spring in my step, I shut off the lights and locked the door behind me. It wasn't the first time I'd closed alone, and I usually got an uneasy feeling of being on the streets alone at midnight. But not tonight. Tonight I was too excited to let that get to me.

I decided against getting an Uber or taking a cab home. I was too excited. Taking a few extra minutes to walk to the train station was exactly what I needed to get some of the energy out.

And now here I am—headed home and lost in my thoughts. I might be an artist—or so I still like to tell myself—but I didn't know much about pulling together a live music night. Ask me to put together an art show and I'll do it for you in five minutes. But music? The idea had me in knots for weeks. But the two acts I lined up for tonight loved the atmosphere and have already asked to play again. One even said he'd tell his buddies about it and try to connect them with me.

I can't take all the credit though. Poor Tori got dragged into this without much of a choice. She had to hear me freak out about it daily and answer my "which flyer do you like better?" questions. I probably owe her lunch just for putting up with me.

Oh! She had a date tonight! That's why she couldn't come in to help. I wonder how it went. I'll have to call her tomorrow and get the scoop. I hope it went well. I need to live vicariously through her.

As I smile at the thought of Tori and her date, I take a second to look around. It's dark and the only light is straight ahead or behind me. This isn't the normal route I take at night.

Shit! I was thinking about so many other things that I accidentally cut down the alley—the one I only use in the daytime. But at this point, if I turn around, I'll miss the train, and I really want to get home and help myself to a celebratory glass of pinot grigio from the finest $7 bottle of wine I could find at the corner market.

I take a deep breath, pull my purse closer to my body, and start up the alley.

During the day, this is a great way to cut my 15-minute walk down to 10, but at night, an extra five minutes is not worth it.

I'm about halfway down, and I can see the intersection at the other end of the alley. I let out a small sigh of relief that I'm almost there.

Crunch. Crunch.

What was that?

I freeze. I know I should keep walking, but I can't. I turn around, but don't see anything.

Must be a rat. That's what I'm going to tell myself.

Knowing damn well I don't want to see a rat tonight, I continue my brisk walk, but before I can take another step, a hand is on my mouth and another arm is around my neck.

Oh my God. Oh my God. Oh my God!

Terror rips through me as the man who is covering my mouth brings me to his chest. I can't see him, but his smell is something awful. I can almost taste the dirt on the hand covering my mouth.

"What's a pretty little thing like you doing out here all alone?" he hisses in my ear. It's not like I can reply. I can barely think right now.

I have no idea what to do. I've never been in a situation like this before. I have pepper spray in my purse, but after the high I was on tonight, I completely forgot to grab it.

As my panic begins to rise, he keeps his hand on my mouth but releases my neck. Before I can wonder what he's going to do next, I feel something sharp pressed against my back.

Is that a knife?

"When I first grabbed ya, I only wanted your purse. But now that I've felt you against me, maybe I should take a little more than that. Want to have some fun tonight?"

He turns and forces me to walk deeper into the alley with him. But when he does, his hand slips from my mouth just a little. And I react.

I bite.

I bite his hand as hard as I can and somehow it's enough for him to loosen his grip on me.

I run.

My small legs are carrying me as fast as they can. I know I don't have much time, but maybe I can get to the end of the alley.

I don't look back. I just look forward. I'm going on adrenaline— that is, until I feel the ground beneath me shift.

A pothole. I didn't see it. I don't think I'm hurt, but it's awkward as I try to get up.

I turn my head to see my attacker now standing over me, grabbing my arms and trying to pull me up. At this point, I'm just flailing and trying to get away, but it's no use; he's way stronger.

But he hasn't covered my mouth again, so I do the only thing left I can think to do.

I scream as loud as my lungs will let me.

4

_____

JAXSON

"**H**ELLLLPPPPPPP!"

What was that?

I'm waiting at a red light a few blocks from the gym, but even over my bike's engine, I can hear a woman screaming. Or at least I think I do. It's faint, but distinct.

I wonder if Abigail was able to scream for help.

I shake thoughts of my little sister from my head. I don't know if what I heard was real, or all in my head, but I can't NOT go and look.

Hoping that whatever I heard was my imagination, I turn the bike off the street and set it against a building next to a dark alley. It's the only place the scream could have come from. It's after midnight, and despite the fact that this is a big city, there aren't many people on the sidewalks.

As I continue up the alley, I see a man straddling something—more like someone. I can't see much because the alley is so fucking dark.

I creep along the edge of a building, trying to stay out of sight. I'm about 30 yards away and the only thing I have on him is the element of surprise. He hasn't heard me or looked around for anything. But as I get closer, I see a woman with red hair on the ground and he's holding a knife to her throat.

Fuck.

I edge closer, trying to do my best to move quickly while not making a sound. She's trying to wrestle away from him, but he's got a knife to her throat, and with every move she makes, she gets closer to having her throat slit.

I don't even think. I just pounce. I couldn't save Abigail, but I'll save someone else.

I jump out of the darkness and rip him off her. Before he realizes what's happening, I kick him in the chin, sending him flying to his back. He drops the knife and I at least have the sense to kick it out of the way. Knowing that he can't reach it, I decide to give his guy a taste of what it's like to be on the bottom, and give him four good punches before I knock him out cold.

It takes me a second to calm down, but then I realize I didn't check on her. Fuck.

When I turn around to look for her, she's gone. As I look up, I see a small figure running toward the street. Away from me.

Red hair. Petite. She looks so tiny I bet I could fit her in my pocket.

Holy shit. Is she the girl from the coffee shop? The sweet tiny redhead I can't get out of my mind?

I don't know why I react to her the way I do. I'm not a relationship guy. I don't date. I scratch the itch when I need to, and usually it's with tall leather-clad girls with jet-black hair who know what they're getting into when they come home with a guy like me. One night. That's it.

This girl? She's definitely too innocent to be sucked into my fucked-up world. She oozes purity and goodness.

I know I should let her run away, but I can't seem to stop myself from calling out to her.

"Hey! Are you okay?"

She turns to look at me and only then seems to realize who I am, because her eyes bug out of her head. I know she's noticed me in the café. I see the way she looks at me when I come in, even though we've never spoken. That's on purpose. If I don't speak to her, I won't be tempted. It's easier to just nod and walk away.

And if I'm not mistaken, those are the first words I've ever said to her.

"Yeah . . . yeah, I'm fine."

But before I can stand up and make sure she's okay, she's turned back around and is racing for the street.

I try to follow her, but by the time I get closer, I see her flagging down a cab.

At that moment, I let out a breath I didn't know I was holding. She might have run away from me like I was the one who attacked her, but at least she's safe.

I saved her. It doesn't bring Abigail back, but at least tonight I won't have another ghost haunting me.

I turn my attention back to her attacker, who is moaning on the ground, slowly coming back to consciousness. I kneel down on one knee and pick up his knife. I place it firmly against his throat as I grab a fistful of his bloodied shirt.

"You show your face around here again, I'll kill you."

5

ANNABELLE

"Wait. So let me get this straight. You were attacked in an alley because you were walking home alone—not cool by the way, and we will discuss that in detail later—and when some guy was holding a knife to your throat, Mr. Dark and Dangerous came out of nowhere and saved the day?"

It's been five days since the attack, but this is the first time I've seen Tori since that night. Her date went a little too well, so she didn't see my message until Sunday. Not wanting to tell her everything over the phone, I promised I'd fill her in during our next shift together.

Once I realized who came riding in on the white horse, I panicked. I should have at least said *thank you*. I shouldn't have run like a freaking coward. But between the attack, and just being near him, my body took over and sprinted to the street.

After I hopped in the cab, all I wanted to do was go home, take a hot shower, and forget about the events of the night. But I knew the responsible thing to do was go to the hospital. I didn't want to file a police report, so I made up a story about falling while I was walking home. Not a complete lie. And they were so busy, the ER bought it without asking questions.

Luckily, there were no cuts from the knife, and I technically *did* fall when I was trying to run away from a freaking crazy robber person. I had some bruises that would take longer than normal to heal, plus a fractured rib. I was ordered to take a few days off from work and get plenty of rest.

I pretty much slept through the weekend, with the events of Friday taking their toll on me. The pain medication didn't hurt either.

"Yeah. Honestly, when I screamed for help, I seriously doubted anyone would hear me, but it was all I could think to do. He saved my life, Tori. And the funny thing is, I still don't know his name."

"I don't know what I'm more mad at: you for walking home alone after midnight with your pepper spray in your purse, or not getting that fine man's name!"

We chuckle. It hurts to laugh, but it feels good at the same time. It means I'm alive. And I know it's not a laughing matter. Leave it to Tori to lighten the mood.

Without a doubt, that was the scariest thing that has ever happened to me in my entire life. I thought I was scared when my mom told me she was diagnosed with cancer. I thought I was scared when she died from it. But even that didn't compare with the utter terror I felt thinking I was going to die in that alley—all because some guy wanted to take my purse.

"Has he been in? Mr. Dark and Dangerous? Have you seen him since?"

I shake my head. "No. And I'm both glad and mad about that. I want to thank him. I feel horrible for not saying it before I sprinted away. But at the same time, I'm sure, like always, I wouldn't know how to talk and would probably blurt out something ridiculous."

"He'll be in. It's not like he comes in every day. But make sure that when he does, you find your voice, Ariel, and thank him. And while you're at it, how about you introduce yourself and ask for his name too?"

I nearly died a few days ago, but apparently that's not stopping Tori from trying to get me to talk to my fantasy man. Or calling me by the name of my favorite Disney princess. I don't know why I'm shocked by any of this.

"Honestly, Tori, this whole situation has put a lot of things in perspective for me. When I told you about it, I felt embarrassed. I know I shouldn't be, but I am. How could I not defend myself? How could I panic and do nothing?"

"You didn't 'do nothing.' You bit and you screamed. From how you described him, he had a foot and probably close to 150 pounds on you. You did what you could do."

"I want to do more. I don't want to feel helpless if I'm ever in that situation again."

That's one of the parts that was hardest to handle with all of this. I've always been small. I'm in decent shape, but I'm not exactly a gym person. But I hated that I couldn't defend myself. It made me feel so weak.

"Well, I might have a solution for you. On my way over here, I saw a flyer for a self-defense class at that MMA gym a few blocks from the café. 'The Pit' I think it's called? Anyway, the class is for women, and the flyer says all skill levels are welcome. Why don't you sign up?"

"An MMA gym? Like those guys who fight in that cage thing? Tori, thanks, I appreciate it, but I don't think I'd be very comfortable there. Maybe I can find a nice one at the Y or something?"

"Annabelle, look at me," Tori grabs my shoulders so she can give me a good staredown. She's kind of frightening sometimes. "You just got done saying you don't want to feel helpless again. Yes, you didn't know how to fight back, but you know what else you didn't—and don't—have?"

I shake my head. All of a sudden, my best friend is getting very real with me and I don't think I like it.

"Confidence," she lets go of my shoulders and rubs my arms. "You're beautiful. And talented. And everyone freaking loves you. But you downplay every compliment. You didn't think you could pull off the new music event, and you blew that out of the water. I've seen your paintings and you are amazing at that. You won't talk to Mr. Dark and Dangerous for Lord knows why. I bet that if you take these classes—do something out of your comfort zone—you won't recognize the girl in the mirror. And that experience will help you not only with defending yourself, but with your confidence. I'll even take them with you."

I hate it when she's right. It's not that I'm not confident—well, okay, fine, I have some self-esteem issues. Who doesn't? But on top of that, I'm just not very extroverted. I'm an artist for goodness' sake, and we aren't exactly social people. Well, at least when it comes to the artists I've met. We're better off in our studios, creating art, not peopling with people.

But the more I think about it, the more I know this is what I should do. Maybe she's right. Maybe I will gain a little bit of confidence. And I'm sure I'll learn enough to feel safe again.

"You'll do it with me?" I might be willing to step out of my comfort zone, but I'll need someone's hand to hold as I do it.

"Hell yeah. I could use some defense moves myself. And I'm sure the eye candy isn't so bad either."

6

JAXSON

The heavy bag I'm doing damage to right now isn't as good as being in the ring, but for today, it will have to do.

Kalum, one of my best friends since we were kids, is holding the bag for me, but apparently, I don't know what kind of power I'm throwing with my punches. After a nasty combination that ends with my patented right hook, he loses his footing and nearly falls on his ass when the bag is too much for him to keep steady.

And that's saying something, because Kalum isn't exactly a small dude.

I take that as a sign that I need a break. Thank fuck these bags can withstand some abuse, because for the last few days, this and my speed bag have taken the brunt of my frustrations.

Since the night I found the coffee shop girl in the alley, my mind has been a fucking mess. Thank God he wasn't able to seriously injure her. If I'm this messed up just from the threat of seeing a woman attacked, I don't know what my brain would be like right now had I not been able to help her.

Maybe I'm in a mood because I haven't had my caffeine fix in a few days. I swear that coffee has crack in it. I've thought about going in, but I don't know how I'd react if I saw her. And I don't know if she wants to see me. I don't want to make her feel awkward, and God knows I'm not exactly the chattiest person on the planet. So I've stayed away. But that doesn't mean I haven't wondered how she's doing.

"What's eating at you, man?" Kalum asks as he takes a seat next to me on the bench. "And don't give me this *nothin'* bullshit. You know I won't buy it."

He's right about that. Kalum and his brother Maverick have been my best friends since we were raising hell on the South Side of Chicago. We might not have been part of a gang, but we knew from a young age that to survive on that side of town, you needed a crew. We were our crew.

Just as I had to live my life knowing I was the spawn of lowlife bookie Stan Kelly, Kalum and Mav's sperm donor was a dealer and a user who died in prison when they were just kids. Hell, I don't even think Mav was five when their old man died. But the streets are tough on that side of town, and as much as we tried to stay out of the life— the life that would put us in 6' x 8' cells—we got pulled in nonetheless.

While my crimes were usually of the disorderly nature, Kalum and Mav had quite the knack for cars. You know the *Fast and the Furious* franchise? That's Kalum and Mav in real life. Or at least *was*. Like me, they got their shit straight in prison, and when they both got out, they opened their own mechanic business.

So, yeah, three fuck-ups from the South Side are now law-abiding business owners. We still can't believe it some days.

I want to tell Kalum to fuck off. I'm not a big talker, even to my best friend, and I certainly don't do this *feelings* shit. But he and Maverick are the only two who know about Abigail, and they won't judge me.

"I've been thinking a lot about Abigail lately."

He drops his head and clasps his hands together. Abigail might have been my blood, but she was everyone's little sister. I never had to worry about her if Kalum and Maverick were around. Hell, I think sometimes they were more protective of her than I was. And that's saying something.

"Why? Is it her birthday? Is it the anniv—"

"No. Nothing like that," I cut him off. "It's just . . . the other night, I was on my way home and heard a scream. A woman—a fucking tiny thing—was being attacked in an alley. Fucker had a knife to her throat. I was able to help her. I kicked the knife away and knocked the guy out cold. I made it more than clear that he wasn't welcome back here, and I don't think he'll show his face again. But all I could think of was: did Abigail . . . did she try to call for help? Could I have helped her?"

Kalum pats me on the back and gives me a few minutes of silence. Those might have been the most words I've said about my sister's death since it happened nearly 12 years ago. She was just a fucking kid—she was 14 when she died.

"You know it's not your fault, right?" Kalum finally breaks the silence. "Your dad's shitty bets and getting in with the worst kinds of guys is why your sister was killed. You have to let this go, brother. Abigail would beat your ass if she knew you were still blaming yourself."

I chuckle, which sounds weird coming out of my mouth because I don't often laugh. Or smile. But he's right. My sister would've at least tried to kick my ass. She might have been seven years younger than me, and I might have towered over her, but she was a feisty thing. God, I missed her.

"I know you're right. It's just not that easy. Maybe I'll let it go. One day. Today's just not that day."

"I get it, man." Kalum hops off the bench and grabs his gloves. "I've got an hour before I have to get back to the shop. Want to go a few rounds?"

I'm a fighter. My dad turned me into one when I didn't have a choice. Though I might have hated him for many things, I did love fighting. But on my terms. It's part of why I opened this gym. I wanted a place to blow off steam where other fighters didn't look at me like I was Stan Kelly's kid. My dad carried a reputation around Chicago's fighting circles—not a good one considering how many people he'd conned over the years—and even though I don't live on the South Side anymore, the fighting community is small. To them, I will always be Stan Kelly's kid.

Lucky fucking me.

Kalum on the other hand? He did it because he knew it was a great workout, and over the years, he realized he needed to be able to hold his own in a fight. He could throw a few punches, and was a decent sparring partner, but I always took it easy on him. He knew it, but we never said that out loud.

"Maybe this time I won't hold back," I say as I adjust my gloves to make sure they are tight around my wrists.

Kalum just laughs. "That's funny. I'm the one who's been holding back on you. I just didn't want you to feel bad. You're known as the fighter in the group. I'm the good-looking one. If I were both, you'd get a complex. I can't have that."

7

ANNABELLE

When Tori suggested signing up for the self-defense class, I was a bit nervous. But the more I thought about what she said, the more I knew I needed it.

I thought I had prepared myself for what I was getting into—going way out of my comfort zone by walking into an MMA gym. I don't know what I'd been thinking, but *this* definitely wasn't what I'd pictured.

When I thought of fighting gyms, for some reason I pictured a dingy warehouse filled with cages and rings. Maybe some guys in the corner jumping rope with an old guy in a gray track suit telling them to keep going.

Fine. I based a lot of what I knew off of *Rocky*.

The Pit *is* in an old warehouse, but it isn't dingy. And I wouldn't have even known it used to be a warehouse were it not for its sky-high ceilings and open floor plan.

We walk in to find a reception desk to our right, but in front of us is a boxing ring, a cage of some sort, and plenty of mats, bags, and equipment. It's masculine without feeling overbearing. It feels . . . strong.

Like I want to be.

"May I help you, ladies?" a man sitting behind the desk asks us since we probably look like deer in headlights. The few times I've been to a gym, the people working the desk look like they're dressed to hit the treadmill at any moment. But this guy is wearing a blue button-down shirt and his hair is styled like he's ready for a date, not a workout.

"We're interested in the self-defense classes. Thought maybe we'd come and check the place out first," Tori says. Thank goodness she spoke. This place is a bit overwhelming, but in a good way.

"Great. We've wanted to offer these classes for a long time, and are glad we could finally fit them in. I'm Reggie, co-owner of The Pit.

"I'm Tori. This is my friend Annabelle. So, Reggie, tell us why we should come here to learn how to kick some ass."

This makes Reggie chuckle, and me too. God love this girl for always knowing what I need.

Reggie begins telling us about the gym, the price of the classes, and that we don't need to be members to take classes. As he begins to walk around the desk, the phone rings, and he excuses himself to answer it.

"This place is huge," I whisper to Tori. I can't help but look around. People are scattered across the gym floor. Two guys are climbing into the ring, and a few women are practicing moves in the cage. It's a lot to take in.

"And I was right about the eye candy. Look who's in the ring."

My eyes shift to the ring, and . . . oh my God. It's him.

What's he doing here? How did I not notice him?

Mr. Dark and Dangerous is in the ring, sparring with another guy who is also quite easy on the eyes. He's shirtless, and for the first time, I can see every tattoo covering his arms and chest. I had dreamed of what he'd look like without a shirt, but this—this did my fantasies no justice.

He's beautiful. Not your classic definition. But as I take in the artwork on his body, the cut of his muscles, and his short brown hair shining with sweat, I can't take my eyes off him. And his eyes are so dark and intent on his opponent. I've never seen anything more mesmerizing in my life.

And the way his body moves when he's in the ring . . . holy shit, I need new panties.

"I know you have dibs on Mr. Dark and Dangerous, but if you ever get his name, get his friend's name too."

"Are you ready for the tour?" Reggie asks, interrupting our ogling.

He shows us around, and the place is just as big as it looked when we walked in. He takes us to the part of the gym that's sectioned off with just mats on the floor and on the wall, which is where the self-defense class is going to be held. I think he talks about the person who will be instructing it, but I hope there isn't a quiz, because I can't stop staring at *him*.

The closer I get, the more I can't tear my eyes away. I've never watched someone fight before, but seeing it up close, seeing how his muscles react to every movement, it's hypnotizing.

I don't even know where we're walking; I just follow Tori. Apparently we've made it back up to the front desk when I feel an elbow in my side.

"Huh? What? What was that for?" I look at Tori, confused.

"Annabelle, Reggie kindly asked if we wanted to sign up, and you didn't answer."

"Oh. Right. Yes. Would love to. Let's sign up. Today."

Reggie chuckles as he passes Tori and me registration forms that we begin filling out. "I get it. It's a lot to take in when you're not used to being around this. I was never a big boxing guy, but this guy right here convinced me to open it with him, and he's a pretty convincing dude."

I look up and see him. I know we call him Mr. Dark and Dangerous, and it's fitting, but sometimes I don't know if it's enough. He's just so much.

"Annabelle, Tori, this here is Jaxson Kelly—somehow one of my best friends and co-owner of The Pit."

I don't think I've blinked. I definitely haven't taken a breath.

Jaxson Kelly.

He has a name. And it's so him. And now he's in front of me, looking at me like I've never been looked at before.

8

JAXSON

U sually when I'm in the ring, I'm completely focused on my opponent, even if I'm just sparring. If you let your focus go, even for just a second, it's the difference between a win and a loss. Or whether you need to go to the hospital. Hell, sometimes it's life or death.

Never lose your focus. Nothing matters outside the ropes.

But when I saw her red hair out of the corner of my eye, I couldn't concentrate. I told Kalum I was done—we had been going at it for about a half hour anyway—but I didn't want to accidentally take a punch. Kalum would never let me live it down if he got one in on me.

I left the ring, threw on a T-shirt, grabbed a bottle of water, and began to take off my gloves when Reggie waved me over.

Christ, did he have to? He always gets a kick out of introducing me to the new female clients. He says it's funny to watch them trip over themselves when they see me—his words, not mine—and I usually give them nothing but a grunt and a head nod.

I really don't want to see her, but that doesn't stop me from walking over to the reception desk. I've been avoiding the coffee shop since the attack. It had been hard to trust myself around her on the

26

best of days. But after seeing her go through something like that? Fuck, it messed with my head.

"Annabelle, Tori, this here is Jaxson Kelly—somehow one of my best friends and co-owner of The Pit."

I nod and extend my hand. "Nice to meet you, ladies. Did Reggie take good care of you? Or did he screw up his one job?"

Reggie just stares at me like I'm growing a second head. He didn't expect me to speak actual words—because, well, I usually don't. I don't do small talk. So hell, even I'm surprised with myself.

I recognize the friend. She works at the coffee shop too. Normally, she'd be more my speed in terms of looks, but for some reason, next to Annabelle, she's just another girl.

Annabelle. Even the name screams "innocent!"

"Nah," Tori said, "Reggie here was great. And now we're all signed up for the self-defense class."

"That's great. Welcome to The Pit. I'm sure I'll be seeing you around."

I turn to leave, and I'm sure if I looked back, Reggie's jaw would be on the ground. Serves the jackass right.

As I head back to the ring to grab my stuff, I almost feel a smile creeping onto to my face. Almost. I don't think I've smiled in more than a decade. I'm glad Annabelle is taking the self-defense class. She held her own that night, but after what she went through, she would have every right to stay hidden and never go out again at night. She's trying to fight back. That's fucking badass of her.

I take a seat on the bench, piling my crap into my duffel bag, when out of the corner of my eye, I see a tiny figure walking over to me. I don't even have to look up to know it's her.

"Hi . . . um . . . Jaxson?"

I barely have to look up to see her. With me sitting, and her being small as hell, I'm nearly eye level with her.

"Hi. Annabelle, was it?"

"Yeah, that's me. I . . . you have a really awesome place here."

"Thanks. It's not much, but it's something to call my own. I figure owning a boxing gym is much better than being an actual boxer."

"Weren't you boxing earlier?"

I knew she noticed me. I don't know why I like the thought of that, 'cause I sure as hell shouldn't.

"Well, yeah, I do it as a hobby. Don't want to make a living getting my face bashed in." I could have added *anymore*, but luckily, my mouth stopped before I said too much. Probably because I hit my conversation limit.

Awkward silence now sits between us. I don't think she came over here to shoot the shit with me, or tell me that she likes my gym. But it's not exactly like I'm used to making small talk—or talking in general—and she's got her nervous-vibe thing going like she does when I go in to get coffee.

"I . . . I wanted to come over here and say thank you. For the other night." She pauses and sucks in a breath, like she needed every bit of air to say those last words. "I don't know how you heard me, or where you came from, but you saved my life that night. I don't know how I can ever repay you."

"You don't need to repay me. The fact that you've come in here, signed up for that class, and are taking steps to make sure you're prepared is payment enough. And not just because I own this place."

She gives me a small smile, and I'm pretty sure it's the most gorgeous thing I've ever seen in my life.

"Well, I want to repay you somehow. Free coffee? I'm sure I could convince my boss to give you free coffee."

I chuckle. Who am I? I don't chuckle.

"Honestly, that's all right. But I do have one request."

I pick up my bag and signal her to follow me to a bench beneath my office.

"Wait here. I'll be right down."

I could have invited her to follow me up, but that would have just been creepy. Yeah, I might check her out when I go get coffee, and I might have saved her from a fucking psycho, but I've just learned her name, and I don't want to scare her.

Annabelle.

She's gorgeous, but I have a feeling she doesn't know it. When she thanked me, those green eyes just about did me in. They were so clear and honest. I couldn't look away. And those freckles sprinkled around her pale skin? Fucking adorable.

She's probably that girl who's had the same boyfriend since the 10th grade and they got perfect grades together. That is, of course, after they were done leading a church group.

Innocent. That's what she is. And she'll stay that way. At least on my part. No one that pure should ever get caught up with the likes of me—a former illegal fighter, ex-con, motorcycle-riding asshole.

I might not be able to have her, but I can still protect her.

I come back down the stairs and hand her the business card I grabbed from my office.

"What's this?" She looks at the card like I gave her a rock.

"You told me you want to pay me back. Here's how. Make me a promise. Promise me you'll never again walk down that alley alone at night. If you're closing alone? You call me. I will come and get you and make sure you get home safe. Deal?"

She stares at it a few more seconds before looking up and smiling at me. God, that smile could end wars.

"Thank you, Jaxson. I promise."

9

ANNABELLE

When I was about six or seven years old, I remember asking my mom about a rainbow. We were at a park in town, it had just rained, and the biggest, brightest rainbow appeared. My mom grabbed her paint supplies and we raced to the park so she could paint the skyline before it disappeared.

"Mommy? What are rainbows?"

I had seen them before, but had never really understood them.

"Rainbows are God's way of telling us that something beautiful can come from even the most horrible storm."

I don't know why that memory has always stuck with me, but it's one of my favorites of my mom and me. Every time I see one, I always stop, look up, and smile. I know that she's not responsible for every rainbow I see, but it always makes me feel closer to her.

The weeks after the attack weren't the big rainbow I saw in the park all those years ago, but they were definitely the bright side of a storm.

The self-defense class at The Pit is awesome. The class is based on Krav Maga, which I had never heard of until I started the course. Apparently, it was developed by the Israeli army back in the 1940s. And it's all about using reflexive responses to threatening situations.

Not only do I feel like I'm prepared if anything ever happens to me again, but I feel strong in my mind *and* my body.

And it feels fucking awesome.

I've started going a few times a week. Tori only goes once a week, but I'm fine going by myself now, which shocked me the first time I did it. Plus there are a lot of great people in the class.

Tori was right—I stepped out of my comfort zone and it was worth it.

Getting to be near Jaxson a few more times a week is an added bonus. He doesn't teach the class, but just knowing I'm in his gym does something to me.

I hear the bell of the Perks door ring, and when I peek out from behind the cappuccino machine I've been cleaning, I see Jaxson standing at the counter. He isn't frowning, which for him is an improvement.

Since I saw him in the gym and properly thanked him for saving my life, something's shifted between us. It's small, but it's noticeable, at least to me. I wouldn't say he's a Chatty Cathy, but he's different. Not as shut off? Warmer? That's a stretch. Not as cold would be a better description. I don't know the words to describe it, but now instead of coming into the café, ordering his usual coffee with his eyes, laying down his money, and leaving, now he actually speaks his order. Sometimes even a hello. One time I swear he flirted with me. Sometimes he smiles at me.

I take what I can get. He still makes me nervous as all get-out, but it's easier than it was a few weeks ago.

"Hey there."

"Hi Annabelle."

God, the way he says my name—I need to record it so I can listen to it on a loop.

"Hi Jaxson. What are you having today? Can I interest you in an Extra Perk half-sweet nonfat iced caramel macchiato?"

Yes, he might not be making actual conversation with me, but that doesn't mean I don't try. It might not be giving him my number like Tori would like, but it's progress. Baby steps here.

He just stares at me for a second. "Is that a real thing?"

Yes! A whole sentence!

"Yup. In fact, the woman sitting over there in the corner just ordered it a few minutes ago if you'd like to ask her for a taste."

What am I saying? Is this my horrible attempt at flirting? God, I am so bad at this. I really need Tori to teach me how to flirt.

I didn't date in high school. It never interested me. The only reason I went to my senior prom—with my gay best friend—was because I knew how much it meant to my mom to be there for me in that moment. We never talked about it, but we knew there was a good chance she wouldn't be around for all my moments, so I wanted to give that to her.

When I went to college, I was either studying or driving back home to be with my mom as much as I could. After she passed away and I moved home, I was just trying to make sure my dad got up and ate breakfast every day. It took him a while, but eventually he got back into his routine: steak and eggs at the same diner every Saturday morning and bingo on Thursdays at the Moose Lodge.

Along the way, I missed a lot of things that normal 20-year-olds experience. Like partying. And dating. And flirting. And sex.

Luckily, Jaxson seems to have found my attempt at flirting, or my reaction to the drink, comical. I hear him laugh. Okay, it was a chuckle. But for a guy who could scare someone with just a look, his laugh might just be the best thing I've ever heard.

He stops abruptly, like he's suddenly realized what he's doing. But that's Jaxson: the man can go from hot to cold in a matter of seconds. Every time I think I'm cracking his walls just a little, he builds them back up.

"Just coffee. Thanks."

"Coming right up."

Though it isn't much, today is the most conversation we have had in—ever? The chuckle took it to the next level. That thought makes me smile. It doesn't take a genius to know he isn't much of a talker. I've never met anyone so closed off, so the fact that he's sharing any words with me makes me feel special.

It makes me crush on him that much harder.
"Here you go. One large black no-frills coffee."
He puts his $5 on the counter and leaves.
Like I said. Baby steps.

10

JAXSON

G od, I was such a fucking asshole.

After Annabelle joined the gym, I started getting coffee again. Figured I'd better get used to seeing her if she was going to be around more. At least that was what I told myself.

I really didn't want to talk to her. Well, I *did*. So fucking bad.

But I couldn't.

I've never been a talker. Growing up where we did, Kalum, Maverick, and I knew that opening our mouths could only lead to trouble. You would either say the wrong thing or slip and say something you weren't supposed to. You were just better off keeping your trap shut. I took that lesson with me when I did my year inside.

When I was a teenager and my old man was teaching me to fight, I learned that if I kept my mouth shut, opponents feared me. And I liked that. No, I fucking *loved* it. I had always been bigger than everyone, but adding a level of fear in the ring, or inside the cage, was never a bad thing. Didn't matter if it was MMA or straight boxing. I was a fighter. And I didn't lose.

Until I lost Abigail.

The only person I ever really talked to was my baby sister. Abigail was the sweetest person to ever walk this earth, and from the moment my mom brought her home from the hospital, I knew this girl would have me wrapped around her little finger.

Somehow, even though she grew up in the same home and neighborhood I did, she didn't let it get to her. She was a straight-A student and was accepted into some fancy-ass private school on scholarship. She wanted to be a social worker. She wanted to save the fucking world. She hated that I fought, but she was just a kid, seven years younger than me, and didn't understand the world of my father's shady deals and illegal gambling that I made sure to protect her from.

Until I didn't.

Annabelle reminds me so much of Abigail. Not in looks. Where Annabelle is tiny with her red hair that I see in my dreams, Abigail had brown hair like mine and would have likely taken after me in the height department.

Considering I'm really fucking attracted to Annabelle, I'm glad she looks nothing like Abigail.

But there are similarities: innocence and purity, plus I wouldn't be surprised if each of them had a halo. Plus both were strong when they had to be. I might not know Annabelle well, but I can tell she's found a strength she didn't know she possessed.

Abigail had no choice but to be associated with me. But Annabelle? I can keep her at arm's length. I have to.

By the time I get back to the gym, Reggie is getting his bag together to take off for the night. He always tries to check out around 4 p.m. He's now a domesticated man and makes sure to be home every night for dinner with his wife and two kids.

When I feel like being an ass, which is often, I tell him he's whipped. He just tells me I'm jealous. But I don't know how you can be jealous of something you've never had. It's not like I grew up in a loving home. My mom did what she could, but with dear old dad being in and out of prison my whole life, it's not exactly like we had a great family dynamic.

"Did I miss anything?" I toss my wallet on the desk and look through the stack of papers Reggie left for me. That's our routine. End of the day before he goes, he leaves me my homework. It might not be a perfect system, but it works.

"Not much. I got the mail. There are a few bills that can wait until later this week. I did put a few invoices in there for you to look over."

"Thanks. Get out of here, man."

Reggie doesn't need to be told twice and turns to leave. I start shuffling through the stack of mail. He was right: bills, junk mail, and a new catalog from an equipment dealer. But there is one letter that sticks out. It's handwritten . . . and addressed to me.

I know that handwriting—those almost unreadable shaky letters I used to see on notes on the counter telling me when and where to show up for a fight. The same writing that used to fill out betting slips that I had to turn in for him, despite the fact that I was only 13.

Stan Fucking Kelly.

Why in the fuck was my dad writing to me from prison? He's toward the end of his sentence for running an illegal fighting ring. He only got eight years because he pled guilty on a few of the charges, so the DA dropped some of the minor ones. It could have been more. Stan was a career criminal, gambler, and bookie, and he would sell you to the devil if it meant saving his own ass.

He only ever cared about making a buck—most of the time, illegally. When he encouraged me to start fighting, I thought it was cool as hell. How many dads told their kids to go punch people?

Then I found out that I was just another way for him to make money. Little did I know, until it was too late and I was in too deep, that Daddy Dearest was operating an illegal fighting ring, with me as the main attraction.

If I never saw that asshole again it would be too soon.

But here I am just staring at the letter. And I'm not going to lie—I feel like it's burning in my hand. All I can do is hold it and wonder what's inside. I don't open it. I can't. I want nothing to do with that bastard.

He ruined my life. He's the reason my sister is dead.

But I don't throw it away. For some reason, I can't. So it goes into the bottom drawer of my desk, where it will likely stay.

11

ANNABELLE

Do you ever have one of those days where you feel like you can do anything? Like you are Leonardo—well, Jack Dawson—on the Titanic yelling that you're the king of the world? You know, before the whole iceberg thing.

That's me today. And I'm not going to lie—it's a pretty damn good feeling.

Last night at the gym, I was finally able to perform a move I'd been struggling with. Being in a chokehold had brought back a lot of memories of that night, so even after almost a month of going to classes, I wouldn't try it. My teacher understood and was super supportive of me.

But last night I was finally ready to work on that technique. It took me a few tries, but soon I wasn't panicking when my attacker grabbed me. I wasn't a master yet, but just getting over that initial fear was huge.

And today, I'm going to get over another fear. I'm going to give Jaxson Kelly my phone number.

Just the thought of it has had me bouncing around all day. I'm usually pleasant with customers and staff, but even I know that today it's a bit much.

"What in the world is up with you today? You're acting like you got laid or something. Oh my God! Did you? Did it finally happen? And if you did, why didn't you call me immediately and report this news?" Tori shrieks.

"Very funny. You know I didn't. Can't a girl just be in a good mood?"

Tori knows I'm a virgin. She's one of the few who does. I didn't mean to tell her, but one night when we'd had a few too many glasses of cheap wine and pizza, it just kind of slipped out when I asked her about giving a blowjob.

After she finished choking on her pizza, I told her that I was a virgin in almost every sense of the word.

I had kissed a few guys, but nothing that I would have written about in my diary. I didn't mean to still be a 23-year-old virgin. It just kind of happened.

I've only had one real boyfriend: Marcus. He lived in a neighboring town and I'd met him at the grocery store. I had heard about people meeting like that, but I never thought it would happen to me. It was cliché as hell when we both reached for the same taco shells.

From there, we began spending time together. He was nice—kind of quiet like me—which made me feel comfortable. We spent a few nights a week together. He said he worked a lot of nights, which was fine. I needed to make sure my dad was okay.

That's why I never spent the night with Marcus. I always felt guilty about leaving Dad, even though he insisted he was fine. Because our nights were always going to end early, Marcus and I never went much further than kissing. He said that he was fine with taking things slow because he really liked me, and I could set the pace for everything we did. I thought it was sweet and considerate.

Until, of course, I caught him with a co-worker at his office one night. I thought I'd be a good girlfriend and surprise him with dinner one Thursday when my dad was at bingo. Seeing him bending some woman over his desk wasn't exactly what I was expecting.

I broke up with him immediately; he didn't even try to fight me on it. Now I'm glad it's over. His cheating gave me the push I needed to move to Chicago.

Once I told Tori all of that, she made it her mission to make sure I lived life to the fullest. For the most part, she does a good job. She's taken me dancing a few times and she's the reason I signed up for the self-defense class. But she hasn't yet been able to get me to open up and feel comfortable around the opposite sex.

But today all of that will change. Today I'm going to take the leap.

Tori just stands and stares at me a bit longer, trying to figure out why I'm nearly jumping out of my apron.

"Okay. Fine. You win. I have no idea why you're acting like you met your celebrity crush. What has my best friend in such a good mood today?"

I can't keep it from her anymore, but I don't want to broadcast it to the entire café. So I lean in and whisper, "I'm going to give Jaxson my number today if he comes in."

"EEEEEEKKKKK. OHHHHHH MY GODDDDDDDDDD!"

So much for that whole "not broadcasting it to the entire café" thing.

Tori grabs my arm and drags me back out of the view of customers. "You're going to do what?"

"I'm going to give him my number."

"How? Why now? I mean, I'm proud as hell of you and have been telling you to do this forever. But why now?"

"I don't know. Today just felt like the day. He's been nicer lately. And he always smiles at me when I see him at the gym. He's even talked to me here. I just . . . I feel like I want to take this leap. I've never felt better about myself."

"Girl," I swear she's crying, "I'm proud of you. Seven months ago, no way would you have done this. Hell, last week I don't know that you would have."

She pauses and gives me a serious look.

"But this is big. Like, you're going from 0 to 100. What if he doesn't call? I mean, he'd be a fucking moron not to call. But I don't want you to get hurt. Putting yourself out there like that is scary as fuck. I always thought for your first attempt at dating, we'd get drunk and put your profile on one of those dating apps and we'd drunkenly swipe left or right, not jump head first with Mr. Dark and Dangerous."

Yes, even though Tori had been the one insisting that we learn Jaxson's name, she still calls him Mr. Dark and Dangerous. Old habits I guess.

But she's right. And I have thought about it, though I haven't been ready to fully admit it.

"I know that giving him my number doesn't mean he'll use it. And I know I have basically no experience with this stuff. But I'm tired of waiting around for things. I moved to Chicago for my life to begin. I've been taking baby steps, and now I'm ready for some bigger ones."

Tori wraps me in a hug and squeezes me a bit too hard, but I don't mind. She's the reason I can do this. I don't know what I'd do without her.

"All right, girl. Let's go give out your digits."

1 2

JAXSON

I t's been a few days since I got the letter from my dad. And even though I shoved it into a drawer to be out of sight, it's not out of mind. Not even close.

Getting that letter from him has been a total mindfuck. I have no clue what it says. Hell, it could be telling me he's dying and has three months to live. That thought actually makes me want to open it.

But I couldn't get that lucky. Stan Kelly will probably live until he's 200 because he made a deal with the devil for his soul in exchange for a $20 knockoff Rolex.

Knowing the letter is in my desk, I've done everything possible to stay out of my office. The staff must wonder what's up with me, because I'm never on the floor this much. I'm not a micromanager. Each person on our team does their job damn well. But apparently my hovering was getting on everyone's nerves so much that Reggie had to kick me out.

I'm glad he did. I could use a walk to clear my head.

Though I haven't opened the letter, I guarantee I know what it says: that he needs money. He's never held down a real job. He's never made an honest living in his life. I don't know if he knows about The Pit, but I guarantee he's looking for a handout.

Over my dead body.

I didn't know where I was walking, but somehow, I ended up in front of Perks. A cup of coffee sounds good, even though I probably don't need to be any more wired than I am right now.

Standing in front of the shop, I can see Annabelle through the window. Her smile is lighting up the entire place as she's walking around talking to customers. I've always been attracted to her, but I can see the subtle changes that have taken place since she's been coming to the gym. She has a little more definition to her body, but is still so feminine and gorgeous.

I've watched her during the classes at the gym. I've hidden, not wanting to seem like some sort of stalker, but I can't stay away when I know she's there. It hasn't come easy for her. She's small, and I don't think she has ever taken a combat class in her life. But the determination in her eyes, and the excitement in them when she catches on to something, is priceless to watch.

I catch her eye as soon as she hears the bell ring when I walk in. The smile she gives me is the most beautiful smile—one that could make any man give up everything—and I can't help but wonder what it would be like to make her smile like that every day.

"Hey Jaxson! How are you?"

"Hi Annabelle. Can I get a coffee?"

"Sure thing. I'll walk back to the counter with you."

I could have made it to the counter in five steps—the place isn't very big, though it's not cramped either—but yeah, I might have shortened my stride to be able to get a glimpse of this beautiful woman from the back.

Yup, that's the ass of someone who's been taking a kickboxing class. I pat myself on the back for putting that back on the schedule.

But I'm a glutton for punishment. That's the only explanation I can think of as to why I'm checking her out, continuing to come in here, when I know I can't have her.

"Your usual?" she asks, snapping me out of my daydream about her ass in my hands as I hold her up against a wall to kiss the ever-loving shit out of her.

"Yeah. Great. Thanks."

She gives me that huge smile again, and I hate that three little words from me can put that kind of smile on her face.

I know she likes me. I might not date, or have ever considered being in a relationship, but I can tell when a woman is interested in me. That hasn't bothered me before. I can tell the difference between the women who just want a good time and the ones who think they can tame the bad boy.

But Annabelle? With the look she's giving me as she pours my coffee? This look is different. It's . . . wanting. Longing. She's picturing us holding hands as we walk down the street together.

Seeing her look at me like that is the second time in my life I've wished for a different path, to be a different person. Because I'm not the guy who can give her what she deserves.

What would it be like? To be that man in her life? I've tried to push down that thought when it's crept into my mind. I don't think she's the kind of woman who would try to change me. She comes to the gym and tells me all the time how much she loves it there. I don't fight for money anymore, so I wouldn't have to keep her away from dark and abandoned warehouses or have to explain why my face is bloodied and bruised.

What would it be like to come home to her after a day at the gym? What does she like to do when she's not working? Would she like to take a ride on my bike—take the day to explore with me? Is she from here? I wonder what her family is like.

And just like that, my fantasy comes to a screeching halt.

Family.

My family. The ones I have and don't have. The reason I could never be with her.

I feel like a bucket of ice has just been dumped on my head.

"Here you go!" she says, breaking me from my thoughts. "Sorry it took so long. I had just put on a new pot, so I was waiting for it to finish so you could have a fresh cup. And . . . well, that's it. Nothing more. See you soon! At the gym. Or here. Or whatever. Have a good day!"

43

"Thanks." I put my $5 on the counter and turn to go. I have no idea why she is rambling and talking in an unusually high-pitched voice, and while it's cute as hell, I need to get out of here. My head is in too many places right now.

As I push open the door to leave, I step out of the way for an elderly woman to walk in. As I wait, I take a sip of the coffee and notice something on the cup. It looks like someone wrote something with a black marker—a big contrast to the normally plain white cup.

I walk out and take a better look. I have to read it three times to make sure I'm seeing things correctly:

Annabelle: 217-555-7926. Grab a drink?

Holy shit. She just gave me her number.

I stand and stare at the cup for what feels like hours. I can't believe she did that. Now the rambling makes sense. She took this huge risk, putting herself out there like that.

And I wish I could do something with it.

Go figure. The five-foot-nothing girl who used to drop trays when I came in now has the balls to give me her number.

And I'm the big fucking coward who is about to break her heart.

I know I can't keep this. It's too much temptation. I need to stay away from her, and she needs to stay away from me.

So I do the hardest thing I've done since I buried my sister—I throw the cup in the trash can and walk away.

ANNABELLE

Joining The Pit was the best and worst decision I've ever made.

The best because I've never been in better shape physically or mentally. What started as just self-defense classes has turned into kickboxing twice a week and a membership.

The worst because I'm now a part of Jaxson Kelly's world. And I pay to be in it.

Since the day I tried to give him my number, he won't even look at me when we're at the gym at the same time, which isn't often, but enough. But I refuse to stop coming here just because the Dark, Dangerous Dickhead is being an asshole.

Yeah, his named changed after the coffee cup incident. I actually came up with it, which made Tori super proud.

My legs have some extra power behind them today as I work out my frustrations on a heavy bag. Just thinking about that day makes me angry.

I had been prepared for him not to call me. I knew it was at best a 50-50 chance. No one goes through life without being rejected, so I'd prepared myself in advance. I figured that if he never used it, at least I took a chance. I'd just hoped it wouldn't be too awkward when I saw him at Perks.

But watching him stop, look at it, and then look at it some more, before throwing it in the trash was a knife to the heart I never expected.

Why was he such an asshole about it? Am I that undesirable that he couldn't even finish his fucking cup of coffee because he wanted to be rid of my phone number so badly?

Wasn't he warming up to me? I thought we had become friends. Well, maybe not friends, but we were friendlier. It took a night of crying, a cheap bottle of wine, and a Tori monologue about why men are trash before my sadness turned into anger.

Apparently, I'm still at that stage, judging by the way I'm kicking this bag right now. But that probably has something to do with him being here today.

If I'm not taking a class, I usually get in here early before work, which has worked out great because I've learned he doesn't come in until late morning. The few times we have run into each other, he hasn't even looked at me. He hasn't come in for coffee. It's like I'm a complete stranger.

And that's what hurts the most.

I mean, he saved my freaking life! He made me promise to call him if I was closing late! He technically gave me his number first! How is giving him my number and asking him for a drink so unwanted?

With one last back kick, I nearly collapse to the floor. I might have gone a little too hard today, but I couldn't stop myself. That's what his presence does to me.

As I stand up, trying to even out my ragged breaths, I look around to make sure he's not on the gym floor. I'm hoping he's upstairs in his office so I can shower, change, and get out of here before I have to see him.

No such luck. He's standing right outside the locker rooms, talking with Reggie.

Deep breaths. I can do this. He's just a guy. Correction: just an asshole.

I give myself a mental pep talk, and with all the confidence I can muster, walk over to the locker room. I have to remind myself not to make eye contact, but when it comes to him, he's like a magnet.

"Annabelle! How you doing?"

Dammit Reggie! Didn't you see I was purposely not making eye contact so you wouldn't talk to me?

"Hey Reggie. How are you?"

That's right. Just Reggie. Take that, dickhead!

"Can't complain. Are you liking it here? I noticed you signed up for a membership."

My eyes continue to stay fixed on Reggie, even though I can feel Jaxson burning a hole through me with his gaze. "Yeah, I'm really liking it. I didn't think this would be something I would enjoy, but I'm becoming addicted to it."

"Glad to hear that. Jaxson, you should see her in the kickboxing class. It's like she's been doing it for years."

I don't want to, but we make eye contact, and I try with every fiber of my being to look disinterested. Or angry. I just hope it's not sadness he sees. I can't let him know how much he has affected me.

His eyes have always been intense. It's what drew me to him that first day he came in for coffee.

But this look? It's intense, don't get me wrong, but there's something more there.

Is it regret? Hurt? Anger? There's so much going on, and I can't make heads or tails of it. I just know that in this moment, I've never been more angry or confused in my entire life.

We stand and stare at each other for seconds, but it feels like minutes. The tension is high. Why? I don't know. It can't be because he has feelings for me. He made that very clear.

Knowing I'm going to snap soon, and I can't let him see me become emotional, I break the silence.

"Well, nice talking to you, Reggie. Jaxson. I need to get to work. Have a good day!"

I all but sprint into the locker room and collapse onto the bench. That's the most I've been around Jaxson since that day, and it's just too much.

He's too much.

I don't want to cry over him anymore, but I can't help it. And I know the tears are silly—it's not like we were dating, but what I felt for him *was* that strong. That real. And I really thought he felt something for me too.

God, I was such a fool.

Not wanting to cry in front of others, I grab my towel and shower kit. I have a long night of work ahead of me; it's another live music night, and I don't want this interaction to dictate my day.

As the steam rises and the tears fall, I make myself a promise: today is the last day I'm going to let Jaxson Kelly be the reason for my tears.

14

JAXSON

I don't know how long the gym has been closed. Reggie left hours ago. I haven't heard anyone in a while. But I can't seem to get up and leave.

Ever since I saw Annabelle today, I've been walking around like a goddamn zombie. I wanted to fucking kill Reggie when he stopped and talked to her today.

I'd been doing just fine avoiding her. I didn't know if she saw me throw away the coffee cup, but I didn't want to find out.

Today told me all I needed to know. She saw. And now she hates me.

Good. Hate is good. I'd rather she hate me. It's safer for her that way.

But fuck . . . that look in her eyes. Yes, there was hate. That was plain as day. But underneath the rage was hurt. And sadness. And I hate that I put those there.

It should go away soon. She'll meet some guy who wears a suit to work every day, brings her flowers just because, and gives her the life she deserves.

A text message interrupts my train of thought. It's Maverick asking me if we're still on for beers tomorrow. At this point, I realize that it's close to midnight.

I shut off the lights, lock the doors, and head for my bike. I really don't want to go home—my loft is better than where I grew up, but it's just a place for me to sleep. I would never say I *lived* there. And honestly, I don't want to be alone tonight. Maybe a ride will do me some good.

I head around the block and pass the coffee shop. I hate that I pass this place every night when I go home. I guess I could take a different route, but I can't seem to make myself do it. Up ahead is the stoplight where I first heard her screams for help. I know that should make me angry, and it does, but now when I think about that night, I think about the woman she's becoming. Not a victim. A survivor.

The light turns green and I shoot ahead, but as I get about a mile from my gym, something catches my eye.

Tiny body. Red hair. A figure that has haunted my dreams.

Annabelle.

Walking alone.

After midnight.

Fuck.

What is she doing out here alone? Hasn't she learned her fucking lesson? She fucking promised me she wouldn't do this!

Before any rational thought enters my brain, I pull my bike over and slam on the brakes. The screech startles her, but I don't care. Serves her right for walking out here alone.

"What the fuck are you doing?"

If I thought she was mad earlier today, what I'm seeing now is unadulterated rage.

"What the fuck am I doing out here? What the fuck are *you* doing scaring the shit out of me? I thought I was going to have a heart attack!"

Does she really not see why I'm mad?

"You're walking home alone! You promised me you would call me if you closed late!" I'm now off my bike, stomping toward her. I can't stop myself. She's now inches away from me and shit, she's fucking sexy when she's mad.

"Oh! Now you care about me!? That's rich, Jaxson. You couldn't even look at me today and now you all of a sudden give a shit about what happens to me? Save it. I don't need your pretend concern. The train station is just a few blocks from here. I'll be fine. You don't need to be my protector anymore."

She starts to walk away, but I grab her elbow. I can't let her go.

"Let go of me. Now, Jaxson."

She's fuming, but so am I.

"Get on the bike. I'm taking you home."

"Like hell I'm getting on a bike with you!"

"So you'd rather do something stupid like walk home alone and get mugged again than get on the bike with me?"

Slap!

She slapped me. I've taken harder hits before, but this one stings like I'll feel it forever.

"Annabelle, get on the fucking bike or I swear to God I will have my ass parked out in front of the coffee shop every night and follow you home. I need you to get on this bike with me. Right. Now."

Knowing I'd make good on that promise, she lets out a frustrated breath and throws her body out of my hold.

"Fine. You can take me home. But on a scale of stupid things I've done lately, this is at the top of the list."

I don't know what hurt worse, that comment or the slap. Both stung. And both were deserved.

I know I shouldn't be mad that she didn't call me for a ride. I wouldn't have either. I've ignored her since she tried to give me her number. I would have told me to go fuck myself too.

But knowing that she was out here alone broke something inside me. The need to protect this girl is like nothing I've ever felt. And although I want her to stay as far away from me as possible, I can't seem to stay away from her, no matter how hard I try.

I give her an extra helmet I carry and make sure it's snapped on tight before I get on. She gives me directions to her place before climbing on behind me.

"Have you ever ridden a bike before?"

She just shakes her head.

"Hold on tight and lean with me. I've got you."

As we drive away, feeling her behind me is better than I'd imagined —her legs pressed against mine, bracing herself for the turns, with her arms wrapped around my waist. She started off not right against me, leaving some space between us. But at some point her front connected with my back, and I felt it all the way through my body.

I'm tempted to take the long way back to her apartment, because this is the best feeling I've had in a long fucking time, and I'm not ready for it to end.

15

ANNABELLE

I am hating every second of this right now.

I hate that he pulled over and stopped me.

I hate that he gets under my skin with his eyes and his voice and his muscles and his tattoos.

I hate how possessive he was when he was demanding to take me home. I hate how much that turned me on.

And I hate how much I love being on the back of his bike.

I got on because I knew he wasn't going to give it up. It's been hard enough avoiding him at The Pit, and somehow I knew he'd keep his promise of waiting for me every night.

I can't see him every day. Not now. That wouldn't be good for my mental stability. Or my wine consumption.

He's the most infuriating man I've ever met. One second, he won't speak to me, then, he's saving my life. Next, he's starting to warm up to me, then *BAM!* he throws away my number and completely forgets I exist. And just when I start to get used to that new normal, he comes out of nowhere demanding that he take me home.

I know I don't have much experience with men, but I have to believe there's not a man on this planet who is as hot and cold as Jaxson Kelly.

We're about 10 minutes away from my apartment. I had been keeping my distance, only getting as close as necessary to hold on to him. But with these last few miles, I'm going to indulge in one last Jaxson fantasy.

I didn't *know* he had a motorcycle, but I figured he did. His whole persona screams "bad boy biker." I had fantasized once about being on a bike with him—riding until we didn't know where we were, and finding a spot where we could watch the sun set. I swung around and sat in front of him, with my legs straddling his, kissing him until we couldn't breathe.

As I'm thinking of all the things I'd like to do with him on this motorcycle, I realize we're on my street.

The fantasy is over.

"Thanks for the ride." That's all I allow myself to say after I take off the helmet. As I take a step away, he grabs my elbow again. Gentler than he did earlier.

"Wait. Let me walk you to your door."

I don't argue, more because I'm now confused and don't trust my words. I'm home. I'm safe. He can sleep just fine tonight knowing I didn't get attacked on the street. What in the world could he still want?

I can't get a read on this man. And once and for all, I'm going to get some answers. No more of this hot-and-cold crap.

"Jaxson, what do you want?" I say as we approach my door.

"I wanted to make sure you got home safely."

"I did. Thank you for that. You drove me home. But you didn't have to walk me up to my door. You could've just dropped me off at the train station, or even in the parking lot, which is 20 feet from here. So I'll ask again: why did you take me home?"

"I told you. Because I wanted to make sure you were safe."

It's like talking to a damn brick wall. And his repetitive answers have my frustration boiling.

And like that, I snap.

"Why do you care? I know, I know, you want me safe. Very noble of you. But if you care so much about my safety, that means in theory you should care about me. So why are you ignoring me? You won't speak to me! Why won't you look at me when I'm at The Pit? Why haven't you been in the coffee shop? And why . . . why did you throw away the coffee cup?"

I suck in deep breaths. Every one of those words has been bubbling inside me for weeks now. Honestly, I can't believe I'm not crying. Anger, apparently, is the winning emotion. The tears I'm holding back are threatening, but I won't do it. I need answers.

When he just stares at me like he has no clue what to say, my resolve crumbles. My anger dissipates. Now this is just defeat.

"Did I do something wrong?" I ask quietly. A tear escapes. "I thought we were at least friends. One minute, you're being nice to me, and the next . . . if you didn't want to have a drink with me, I would have understood, but . . ."

Before I can finish, his lips are on mine, silencing my words.

This kiss is like nothing I've ever experienced. It's hot and it's desperate, but it's also controlled and firm. It's everything.

Before I can sink into it, he pulls away as quickly as it happened.

"You think I wanted to hurt you? You don't think I *know* how much I hurt you? Fuck, Annabelle, however much you're hurting, multiply that by 100, baby, because that's what I've felt since I first laid eyes on you."

I'm stunned.

He's hurting?

He wants me?

Did he just call me "baby"?

"I don't understand."

He takes my shoulders and looks down at me. Our eyes are connected, like we both know that these words are the most important we'll ever say to each other.

"Since the moment I saw you, I've not been able to stop thinking about you. Want to know why I didn't talk to you when you first started working at the coffee shop? Because I didn't trust myself around you. And my world is not one you should be a part of. I'm not a good man, Annabelle. I've done things I'm not proud of and you are too good—too pure—to be around some asshole like me. Me acting the way I did? That was for your own good. You deserve someone way better than me."

"My own good? What gives you the right to decide what is right for me?"

"I don't have the right! But see? That's me. I'm a selfish bastard. I kept coming in to see you, because I couldn't fucking stay away. I pulled over tonight because the thought of you alone at night drove me fucking insane. But I know I can't have you! Me throwing away the coffee cup? That was me throwing away the temptation of calling you. You are a fucking temptress, Annabelle, and I can't stay away."

"I don't want you to."

Our lips clash in a frenzy. I didn't know a kiss could be more desperate than the one he gave me just minutes ago, but somehow, this is.

We are nothing but lips and tongues and hands grabbing whatever we can to be closer to each other. I'm on my toes to reach him, which apparently isn't enough, because before I know it, he's picked me up and has me pinned against the door. I instinctively wrap my legs around him, loving the feel of how close we are.

My hands go around the back of his neck, holding on tight, but also knowing that he won't let me fall. At least not this way.

At some point the kiss slows, but it's still filled with need. He has one hand underneath me to hold me up, but the other begins trailing up my body, brushing the side of my breast. Just this small touch is enough to do me in, and I arch into his touch. Like he already knows how to make my body sing, he brings his hand back down to lift up my shirt, and guides the same hand back up, only this time to take me in his hand.

I've always hated my chest. I'm one of those girls who's petite everywhere. But Jaxson doesn't seem to care. The way he's massaging my breast and playing with my nipple is turning me on in ways I didn't know possible.

"Jaxson . . ." I say in a breathy moan. I'd needed air, and as soon as I had it, his name was the only thing I could say.

I wish I hadn't. With the sound of his name, it's like I've snapped him out of a trance. Before I know it, he's putting me down and backing away.

"No, Jaxson, don't go. Please don't go." I'm grabbing for him. I'm desperate. I can't let him leave.

"I can't, Annabelle. I can't do this to you. This was a mistake. Stay away from me, and I'll stay away from you. It's for the best."

He turns and walks back to his bike like the last hour didn't happen.

And I'm left standing in front of my building—turned on, confused, and heartbroken knowing I'll never forget the last hour of my life.

JAXSON

My fists are flying like I took speed before a fight. The combinations are exiting my body without much thought behind them.

1-2-5-2...

1-2-3-2...

I'm not thinking; I'm just going on adrenaline. I don't even know who the fuck my sparring partner is, and unfortunately, I don't feel bad for the bastard who's taking the brunt of my frustration.

Since last night, I haven't been able to think of anything but Annabelle. Her lips—God, they tasted sweeter than I thought they would. Her skin was so fucking soft. Her body. Shit, her body was fucking made for me. How perfectly it fit against me when I had her pinned against the door. Just like I had imagined.

I had no right to kiss her like that. God, I wanted to take her inside her apartment and claim her. Make her mine.

But I have no business even thinking that. I had my taste of her. That will have to be enough.

1-6-3-2...

The last combination knocks my sparring partner into the ropes, and before he can get his balance, he falls to the canvas. Blood is dripping from the corner of his mouth and he looks like he's seeing three of me.

Fuck.

I just stand in the ring, silently berating myself. I never get that intense with a sparring partner, especially one I've never gone rounds with. But today I just needed someone to go against; a bag wasn't going to do. Stupid kid said he could hang.

"Jaxson! Fuck, man. Get the fuck out of the ring. Now."

I don't trust myself inside the ropes anymore, so I listen to Reggie and climb out. As soon as I find the bench, I hang my head with my elbows on my knees.

I don't get out of control like that anymore. Those punch sequences I'm pretty sure I was throwing? Those were from my fighting days—when I had one job, and that was to leave my opponent on his ass.

"When you pull yourself together, I'll meet you in your office and you can tell me why you almost killed one of our clients."

Reggie walks away and I don't even bother arguing with him. I know he's right. I can't be in the ring, or hell, even in public, when I'm worked up like this.

Maybe I need a few days away. Clear my head. Take the bike and just ride. Put some space between myself and the temptation of Annabelle and all things that remind me of her.

It's not like I have anything keeping me here. Reggie could watch the gym for a few days. Kalum and Maverick wouldn't question it if I said I needed to get away. I don't see my mom as much as I should, so I doubt she'd even know I was gone.

Yes, that's what I'm going to do. Maybe putting a few days, and a few hundred miles, between us is what I need to kick my Annabelle habit. Because after just one taste, I became addicted.

When I walk into my office, Reggie is already sitting, legs kicked up on my desk.

"Want to tell me why you were throwing punch combinations meant to put someone in the ER?"

I take a seat across from him, knowing I'm about to hate whatever conversation he wants to have with me.

"I wasn't trying to kill a client; I just got carried away. I'll go apologize to him. Give him a month free considering I busted his lip open."

Reggie just stares at me. He knows I'm deflecting. We might have only known each other for a few years, but the man can read me like a book.

"How about you try that again? Why were you fighting like you wanted to kill someone?"

I sigh. While I'm not exactly a guy who talks about feelings and shit, Reggie might be the only person I know who might get what's going through my head. Kalum and Mav, though we grew up in the same shit neighborhood and all at some point served time, are eternal bachelors who are all about fast cars and faster women.

"Do you ever think you're not good enough for Lisa?"

This makes him chuckle, and though it doesn't answer his question, he gets that this is how I need to begin.

"Every day, man. Every fucking day."

We sit in silence for a bit—neither of us quite knowing what to say, or how to say it.

"Did I ever tell you how I met Lisa?"

I shake my head.

"It was the day I got out of prison."

Damn. I didn't know it was that quick. I just knew that in the three months I didn't talk to him between our release dates, he went from a single guy talking about how many girls he was going to fuck when he got out, to being completely pussy-whipped.

"I pulled petty crime shit all my life. Never got caught. Honestly, it was more about the rush than actually needing whatever I was grabbing—that is, until I got bold and tried to break into the safe at the bank I worked at. I wasn't a bad guy, but I wasn't one you brought home to mom, you know?"

I nod my head, relating to that statement more than he probably realizes.

"The day I got out, I didn't know who I was. Yeah, you and I were talking about opening this place up, and I didn't feel like a *bad* guy, but it hit me when I drove away from prison that I was officially an ex-con. I ended up at this diner and I don't know how long I just sat there, really thinking about stuff."

He takes his feet off the desk and sits up straighter. But as he does, he smiles the smile he has when he talks about his wife.

"I was so in my head I didn't even notice Lisa when she took my order at first. Later, she asked me if I wanted another cup, and something about her voice made me look up. She was the most beautiful girl I'd ever seen, and that wasn't because I had just done three years with a bunch of dudes."

We chuckle.

"We talked her entire shift. Basic shit. Some flirting. But at some point, I realized she didn't know me as an ex-con. She knew me as me: the person I wanted to be. Eventually, I told her about my past, because I knew I wanted a future with her. She made me want more than I ever thought I deserved, and she showed me that I deserved happiness, in spite of my past."

I nod, his words hitting me in the gut.

"Did she treat you differently when you told her about your past?"

"Honestly, she had an idea. I'd told her I didn't grow up in the best neighborhood, so I think she suspected. But she told me, without a doubt, that as long as I left that life behind me, she'd help me keep it there."

I let his words sink in. He makes it seem so easy. Honestly, Lisa is great, and his two kids are awesome. And he's happy. Content.

And honestly? I'm jealous as fuck.

I want that. The wife. The family. The something to come home to every night. The little boy I could teach to throw a football and the little girl I could scare boys away from.

But could I really have it?

"Listen, I don't know what's going on with you, man, but I see the way you look at Annabelle when she comes in. I see that look in your eye. I don't know why you haven't made a move, or what's holding you back, but if you listen to anything I've ever said to you, listen to this: you control your future. No one else. Nothing in your past has to dictate your tomorrow. So the question is: what are you going to do about it?"

He gets up, leaving his final words to settle, and walks out of the office.

I know he's right. He's so fucking right.

Now I just need to man up and do something about it.

17

ANNABELLE

"Whoa, girl. What did that counter ever do to you?

Tori's words startle me, but then I realize I've been wiping down the same spot for I don't even know how long.

Sadly, this isn't the first time this week she's had to do that.

It's been four days since Jaxson kissed me. Four days since I felt his lips on mine. Four days since I felt his rough hands hold me like I've never been held before.

He's kept his word about staying away from me. I've only been to The Pit once, and he wasn't there. He hasn't come in for coffee.

"It's for the best."

Those are the words that have been rolling over in my head every minute of every day. What does that even mean? It's not like we tried to date and it didn't work out. Hell, I barely know anything about him!

I was sad the day after. I called Tori, she brought over ice cream, and I got all my tears out—you know, the tears I said I'd never cry for him again.

Now I'm back to being angry. And apparently I'm taking it out on our café counters.

"Maybe we should go out tonight? I can cancel my date. Maybe you just need a night to dance it off?"

I put down the rag and look at my best friend. I know she's been excited for this date all week. Just because I'm miserable doesn't mean she has to be.

"No, you go. I'm fine. I'm off tomorrow. I'll go to the gym really early, take all this out on a heavy bag, and be good as new."

"Are you sure? Because chicks over dicks. All day every day. I would totally canc—"

Tori's words trail off as her eyes go wide. She's facing the door, and I can't imagine who could be walking in to make her go speechless like that.

Her eyes beg for me to turn around, and I'm not expecting who I see standing in the doorway.

Jaxson.

We're about ready to close, but it was slow tonight, so everyone has already taken off. It's just Tori and me . . . and now the man who has been haunting my dreams.

The only noise in the café is the soft music we always play and the hum of the machines we haven't turned off yet. I don't know why he's here. Wasn't he the one who said he needed to stay away?

Nope. Fuck this. He can't keep coming around and screwing with my heart. It's not fair to me.

"You need to leave."

My words shock both Tori and Jaxson. They shock me too. I've never been this outspoken, but this roller coaster he keeps putting me on has to stop, and apparently, it's made me say what's on my mind.

"Annabelle, I want to talk."

"What do you want to tell her?" Tori has now taken a slight step in front of me. Always my defender.

"That's between Annabelle and me. I want to explain. I need . . . I need to talk to her."

I can hear the hesitation in his voice. It's almost like he's scared. But between how he's looking at me, and the words I know were so hard for him to say, I feel my resolve crumbling.

A chirp breaks the silence: a text on Tori's phone.

"Fuck. It's Andrew. He'll be here in five minutes."

I look at her, then him. His eyes—those deep brown eyes—are all but begging me for this. And I'm not strong enough to deny him that.

"It's okay. Go. I want to hear what he has to say."

"Are you sure?"

"Yes. Go. I'll call you later."

Tori grabs her purse from behind the counter and marches to the door, but stops in front of him before she leaves.

"This is your last chance, asshole. If I find her crying again tonight, you will lose body parts. You hear me?"

He nods, but doesn't promise anything. I think we both know that's a promise neither of us can keep.

Tori exits the shop, leaving Jaxson and me staring at each other. He eyes a table, and we go to sit. I refuse to speak first. He came here. This is on him.

"I don't know where to start."

At least he broke the silence first.

"Tell me why you're here."

He sighs and takes a breath, gathering the strength to say his next words.

"When I told you I'm not a good man, Annabelle, I'm not. I come from the South Side, and I was in and out of trouble my whole life. Real trouble . . . I've done hard time. And I'm a fighter. I've fought since I was a teenager."

"I know you're a fighter, Jaxson. I don't have to know boxing to tell you're very good at it."

He grabs my hands, and I let him. I can tell he needs this, and I want to be the one to give it to him.

"When I was a kid, my dad started teaching me to fight. Just the basics. But then he started setting me up to fight with guys at this gym, and I liked it. I felt like a badass. Pretty soon, he started taking me to fights. He was always making bets and talking to people, and for me that was normal. I thought it was cool. Then I started fighting in those fights. And I won. I always won. Which I didn't find odd because I knew I was good."

He trails off. I don't know how many times he's told this story, but I have a feeling I'm one of the few to ever hear it.

"One day, I overheard my dad on the phone. Stan's his name. I heard him talking about fixing my fight . . . saying that I was too dumb to realize what was going on. He was fixing my fights, Annabelle. He was using me for his illegal gambling and taking bad bets because he was rigging the outcome without my knowing."

I squeeze his hand. I know that I hit the lottery when it came to parents, so it's hard to fathom how a dad could use his son like that.

"I was furious. I didn't know what to do. I thought I was winning that entire time. I didn't know what was real anymore. Then, before my next fight, I confronted him about it. Told him I knew he was fixing fights and that I was out. I was done. He could find someone else to make money off of; it wasn't going to be me. I walked away, Annabelle. I told my dad to go fuck himself and I got on my bike and left."

I bring his hands to my lips, not knowing what to say, but needing to show him how proud I am of him. Not just for leaving that world, but for sharing this with me.

"Jaxson, that doesn't make you a bad guy. So what if you fought? So what if it was illegal? You didn't know what you were doing. Now, you haven't gotten to the part where you tell me about jail, but we can get there another time. I don't see how this makes you a bad guy. In fact, I think this makes you brave, because you chose to get away from that situation."

My words dangle in the air. I know there's more, but right now, I'm not sure what to expect.

"I had a sister. Abigail. She was 14 when I found out about all of this. You remind me of her in some ways. Sweet and innocent, but possessing strength that can't be taught. Anyway, the night I walked away, she was walking back late from the library. She was smart. So fucking smart. I usually went to pick her up, but after I walked away from the fight, I was so out of it I completely forgot."

66

I know what's coming next. I can feel it. And God, I hope I'm wrong.

"She died that night because of me. Because I didn't fight, a bunch of guys who placed bets lost a lot of fucking money because of my dad, and they were waiting for him at our place. She didn't know what she was walking into. Those assholes apparently thought attacking an innocent kid was required to show my dad that they weren't fucking around when it came to their money."

I can't take it anymore. I get out of my seat and sit on his lap, wrapping my arms around his neck and bringing myself as close as I can. I don't know what to say. I just hope this gives him what he needs right now.

"If I had been there that night, she wouldn't be . . . If I would've fought that night . . ."

I grab his chin so I can look in his eyes. I need him to hear these words.

"Jaxson. Look at me. It's not your fault. If anyone should be living with guilt, it's your father. You couldn't have known what would happen that night."

"It's my fault, Annabelle. My sister is dead because of me, and I'll never forgive myself for that."

Not knowing what else to say to make him understand that none of that changes the way I feel, I bring my lips to his.

This man. The way he just opened up to me, telling me what he deals with on a daily basis—I get it now. I understand his *why*. I get why he freaks out when I walk home alone, and though I don't agree with it, I understand why he thinks he's protecting me.

But I don't care about any of that. If anything, I want him even more now.

"Jaxson?"

He brushes a stray piece of hair behind my ear. "Yeah, baby?"

Yup. That sealed it. Hearing that term of endearment leave his mouth has broken the last wall around my heart.

"Thank you for sharing that with me."

He adjusts me so we're looking directly at each other.

"I can't stay away, Annabelle. I need you. So much."

I stand up from his lap and go grab my purse and keys. When I walk back to him, feeling bold, I circle my hands around his neck and place a light kiss on his chin.

"I have to close up, but I'm all alone. Will you take me home, Jaxson?"

Before I know it, I'm on the back of his motorcycle knowing my life is about to change forever.

18

JAXSON

I don't know what it is about this girl, but when I'm with her, I barely recognize myself.

I've never told my whole story to anyone. Not Reggie—hell, not even Kalum and Maverick know everything. They know enough, but the details that I just shared with Annabelle were the secrets I carried with me.

But once I started talking, it was like I couldn't stop. The dam broke, and the words poured out. And I'll admit, I felt relief getting everything out there. Like the burden I've carried had somehow been lifted.

The way she looked at me, the way she let me set the pace, knowing this was hard for me, made me fall that much harder. She knew exactly what I needed.

And now, I need her.

As I walk her up to her building door, I don't stop. I let her lead me. If she wants me to come up with her, I won't deny her that. I won't deny myself that.

I need her. Whatever she'll give me, I'll take.

We take the stairs up to her second-floor apartment. Her building is in decent shape, which makes me feel better—at least she doesn't live in a shithole.

She fiddles with her keys and struggles to open the door. I place my arms around her waist, and place a kiss on her shoulder. This seems to calm her, and she opens the door to her apartment.

The small space is so her. Tons of color, but not so much that it looks chaotic. Furniture that you can tell is second-hand, but has been restored. A painting of a park with a rainbow catches my eye above her full-size bed. It's a small studio, but she seems to use the space well.

"I . . . Can I get you . . . Would you like something to drink?"

Her nervousness makes me smile, because though I might not be showing it, I'm nervous too. Not for whatever might happen tonight, but for what could happen after.

I take her hand and guide her to the couch. I want to put her at ease. I'm in no rush for the physical stuff. Hell, I haven't even taken her on a proper date. I can at least do that for her.

"Come sit by me."

She listens to my quiet demand and sits next to me on the couch. But instead of crawling into me like she did at the café, she sits with space between us.

That won't do.

I turn to face her, closing a little of the distance, and take her hand in mine, needing to touch her in any way I can.

"I don't know what's going through that pretty head of yours, but whatever you're thinking, you can tell me. You now know more about me than anyone on the planet, so it's only fair."

She won't look at me. The girl who confronted me earlier and demanded I give her answers has now been replaced by this shy beauty.

"I want to kiss you. But I'm not very . . ."

All I heard was *kiss*, and I became a man possessed.

I direct her to my lap so she's straddling me, and I claim her mouth like I've wanted to every day since the first time I got a taste of her.

That first kiss outside her building was desperate—like we were taking something we knew we weren't supposed to have.

This? This kiss is determined. Deliberate. Every movement of our lips, every sweep of our tongues, is purposeful—showing what we mean to each other.

And if I have my way, I'm never going to have another woman's lips on mine again.

She lets me set the pace, following me with every movement. I can tell she's still nervous, but I don't want her to think. I just want her to feel.

I break away from her lips and begin a trail of kisses down her neck, then down her shoulder, as my hand goes under her shirt. I'm dying to touch her perfect tits again, but I don't want to rush this.

"We only go as far as you tell me, baby. I'm not going anywhere," I reassure her as my hands feel the soft skin of her stomach and my lips continue light kisses anywhere I can find skin.

"More, Jaxson. I want more."

Taking that as my opening, I lift her shirt over her head. She's a vision. Her pale blue lace bra is taunting me against her creamy skin. Her tits aren't too big, but enough to fill my hands, which is plenty for me to work with. Freckles are scattered across her chest and I want to kiss each and every one of them.

As my lips trace the top of her chest, she begins to squirm on top of me. I can tell this is turning her on, so I don't let up. I want to learn every single thing that drives her crazy.

I take a nipple in my mouth through the blue lace, and as I begin to suck on it, her hips buck against me. If I wasn't hard before, I'm now a fucking stone. Between the confines of my jeans, and her pressed against me, my cock is begging for relief.

But it can wait. Right now, the only thing on my mind is making this woman scream in pleasure.

I pick her up and lay her on the couch, taking off her bra before I lay her down. The couch is so small that I can't fit on it with her, but that's fine. I can work with this. She's a vision as she looks up at me as I kneel next to her—lust in her eyes, wanting everything I'll give her.

I take my hand and cup her pussy. I can feel the heat of her center through her jeans, and fuck if it isn't making me insane.

"Yes, Jaxson! Feels so good . . ."

"Are you wet for me, baby?"

I know she is, but I'm dying to hear her say those words to me. But all she can do is nod her head.

"Hmm, I'd better find out for myself then."

I unzip her jeans as her hand rubs up and down my arm. It's reassuring that she's in this with me.

When I get her jeans off, I can't help but smile. A pair of panties that match her bra greet me, and as I lift up her legs to slide the jeans off, I can already tell this girl is wet and ready for me.

"Fuck, baby. You are so wet. I need to feel it."

"I'm yours, Jaxson. Make me yours."

I pull her panties down harder than I intend to, but those words have lit a fire under me. Her small strip of hair is like a siren calling to me. I feel around her wetness before slipping in a finger.

Fuck, she's tight. And fucking perfect.

Her hips buck against my finger, like she's shocked about the entrance. But I can tell she likes it. She's already riding my finger, chasing her orgasm that I'm bound and determined to give her.

"Do you like that, baby?"

"Jaxson . . . I . . . yes . . . more!"

I've never wanted to give someone something so bad. My finger continues to go in and out, searching for the spot that will make her scream. As soon as I hit it, I can feel her body shift underneath me.

"Oh my God, Jaxson!"

Wanting to give her more, I swing her legs so they are on either side of my head. Still kneeling on the floor, with her legs on my shoulders, I'm at the perfect angle to taste what I'm craving.

"Baby, I need to taste you."

She doesn't reply before my tongue finds her center and *FUCK*, I've never tasted anything better in my life.

As my tongue licks the sweetest pussy I've ever tasted, I take my hand and rub circles around her clit, which is making her thrash beneath me.

"Jaxson . . . I . . . what is . . ."

"Just let it happen, baby. Let me take you there."

With a few more strokes and one last suck of her clit, she explodes. Her juices are covering my face, and God, I fucking love it.

As she tries to control her breathing, I find her bathroom and grab a washcloth. My cock is screaming at me for some relief, but it can wait.

What I just experienced was like nothing I've ever had.

When I come back to the living room, she's still half-sitting, half-lying on the couch. She looks relaxed and so fucking gorgeous as she lets me tend to her.

"Jaxson?"

I look up at her. "Yeah, baby?"

"Take me to bed. Make love to me."

ANNABELLE

I can't describe this feeling right now. It's like nothing I've ever felt in my life.

I'm coming down from my first orgasm ever. And it was from Jaxson.

And, oh my God, if that's what an orgasm is, then I've been missing out. But somehow I have a feeling it's because of him.

The way he touched me was like he knew what my body wanted better than I did. Which is good, because I had no idea what I wanted —well, not specifically, but I did know I wanted him.

And I still do.

As he comes back into the room, holding a washcloth, my heart melts. This big, strong, brooding man is now kneeling in front of me —again—taking care of me—again—after I've done nothing for him.

A few times when I'd fooled around with Marcus, he would take my hand and subtly urge me to give him a handjob. I never did; I never felt comfortable enough.

But not Jaxson. This man gave me everything and asked for nothing in return.

And now I want to give him all of me.

"Jaxson?"

He looks up at me, giving me a questioning look like he's wondering if I'm regretting what we just shared.

"Yeah, baby?"

"Take me to bed. Make love to me."

My words shock him. Honestly, they shock me too. I know we've just figured things out. Hell, I don't even know if we've done that yet. But I know, more than ever, that this is the first man I want to be with.

No matter how long this relationship lasts, no matter what happens, I want Jaxson Kelly to be my first.

"Are you sure? Baby, we don't have to do this."

I nod my head. "I want to. I want to feel you, Jaxson."

With that, he picks me up, cradling me against him, and carries me to the bed. He places me down gently, like he might break me if he lets me down too hard.

I'm now sprawled before him, completely naked. He's standing over me, with every bit of clothing on.

"I think you're overdressed," I say to him as I trail a hand over my chest and down to my pussy.

I don't know where this wanton woman is coming from, but I like her. She's sexy and confident. A woman worthy of Jaxson.

The look he's giving me is hunger. Like he's starved for me, and I'm about to be his last meal.

He frantically begins undressing, grabbing a condom from his wallet before he tosses his jeans to the side.

I got a taste of what he looked like underneath his clothes when I saw him shirtless at the gym, but that was nothing compared to what I'm seeing now.

There are tattoos strategically placed all over his body. They are beautiful. I all of a sudden have an overwhelming urge to lick every inch of ink that covers his body.

His chest is smooth, with abs so defined they look like a sculptor made them, and there's a small trail of hair leading down to his—*oh my God!*—he's fucking huge.

I knew he would be. He's so big everywhere else, why would his dick be any different? I'm now all of a sudden nervous. How in the hell is he going to fit?

I haven't told him I'm a virgin and I'm not going to. He'll stop this if he knows. I know he will. And there is nothing I want more than this. Right here. Right now.

"You look absolutely gorgeous," he says as he lowers himself next to me on the bed. His hand replaces mine at my center, as he begins working me again. I'm convinced that nothing will ever feel as good as his hands on me.

I pull him into me, needing to feel his lips on mine. He responds, rolling me over so he's on top, kissing me like we've done it for years. It's amazing that we've just gotten together—we're already in sync with each other's movements.

My first kiss with Marcus was awkward and sloppy. We butted heads a few times because we didn't know which way the other would go. Not Jaxson. Kissing Jaxson is as natural as breathing.

Without thinking, I move my hand down and begin to stroke his cock. It's so big and hard, and it twinges at my touch. Feeling that he responds to me like that turns me on all that much more.

"Jaxson, please. I want you . . ."

He stops his kisses, stroking my hair back while looking down at me. "Baby, we don't have to. I never expected it to go this far when I came up here. This is enough for me."

"I know. But I want you," I know I'm pleading, but I can't help it. "I've wanted you for so long. Don't make me wait any longer."

And he doesn't. He grabs the condom, slips it on, and positions himself on top of me.

He kisses me again as he lines up with my center, and I don't know what I expect to feel when he enters me, but it's definitely not this.

A sharp pain. I knew it would hurt; I'd been told numerous times it would. Unfortunately, I flinch, and Jaxson takes notice.

"Are you okay, baby? Did I hurt you? We can stop."

I shake my head. "I'm okay. Please, Jaxson, keep going. I want this."

He takes it slow, and after I adjust to his size—holy shit! I don't have words. The feeling of him inside me, moving in and out at a pace that's not slow, but not rushed, is the most amazing thing I've felt in my life. The way he's filling me is nothing I could describe and everything I didn't know I wanted.

"More . . ."

I don't know where that came from, but my body wants it. Is craving it. He listens, and pulls one of my legs up so he can go deeper.

And God, does he.

I don't even realize I'm doing it, but soon my body is meeting his thrusts and silently asking for more. I feel my orgasm coming again, but it's still out of reach.

"Fuck, Annabelle. You're so fucking tight. So fucking perfect. I'm not going to last much longer, but I need you to come again."

"Yes, Jaxson. Please."

He takes both of my legs and puts them on his shoulders and *holy fuck* I don't know what spot he's hitting, but it's . . .

"AAHHHH!!!!"

I explode. I'm seeing stars. I'm grabbing for anything I can hold on to as my body convulses in pleasure.

And before I know it, I feel Jaxson tighten inside me, and he follows my orgasm with his own.

We collapse on the bed, him on top of me, spent from the night.

I don't know what tomorrow is going to bring, but I hope it's more of that. Because that's what I've been waiting for.

20

JAXSON

A slice of daylight wakes me from the best sleep I've had in who knows how long.

And it has everything to do with this beautiful woman next to me.

Being with Annabelle last night was everything and nothing I could have imagined—the way her body responded to mine, and the little moans that drove me fucking wild. Not to mention her tight-as-fuck pussy gripping the life out of me.

The recollection of how she screamed when I gave her that last orgasm will be something I'll have burned into my memory until the day I die.

If I thought she was beautiful before, what I'm seeing now, with her lying next to me . . . I don't have words to describe it. Without an ounce of makeup, her hair a mess, and her body completely naked under the sheets, she's a vision I don't deserve to take in.

I don't know why she wants me, or why she thinks I'm worthy of her, but I know without a shadow of a doubt, from this point forward, that I'll do everything I can to be the man she needs.

I do my best to roll out of bed without disturbing her, the bathroom calling my name. After we had sex, we both crashed hard—the day and the emotions having caught up with both of us.

As I come back into the room, I can't help but stop and look at the woman who I somehow am going to be able to call mine. She's now sleeping on her side, and all I want is to be the "big spoon" and feel her warmth.

I've never been a cuddler. Hell, this is the first time I've spent the night with a woman. But the need to hold Annabelle in my arms is overpowering right now.

I walk back to the bed and lift up the covers, and that's when I see a dark red spot clashing with her cream-colored sheets.

Is that . . . is that blood?

My body goes cold as I look at the small stain.

Is she?

Was she?

What the hell?

Fuck, she was tight, but . . .

Oh my God.

How could she not tell me she was a fucking virgin?

Fucking shit. I took her fucking virginity last night and I had no fucking clue.

I pause, realizing it could just be her time of the month. I'll let her explain instead of jumping to conclusions.

Like she can hear the thoughts racing through my mind, she turns to me, slowly waking up.

"Good morning," she says as she wipes the sleep away from her eyes. "Have you been up long?"

It takes all I have to not snap at her before she's even fully awake. But I'm going to get some fucking answers.

"Annabelle, I need to ask you a question, and you need to tell me the truth."

My sharp tone startles her awake, and she gathers the sheets to cover her chest as she sits up to look at me.

"Last night . . . before we . . . Christ . . . Were you a virgin, Annabelle?"

She can't hide her reaction. The panicked look on her face says it all.

"Fuck, Annabelle! How could you not tell me? That's something really damn important I should have known before we . . ." I can't even think straight and I'm now pacing around her small apartment. I'm freaking out.

I wasn't good enough for her before, but I definitely shouldn't have been the one to pop her cherry.

"I knew you wouldn't if you knew."

Her words come out as a whisper, making me wonder if I heard her correctly.

"What was that?" I'm really trying to keep my temper down, but this whole thing has thrown me for a fucking loop.

She finally looks up at me, and it guts me to see a single tear falling down her cheek. It takes all I have to not jump onto the bed and wipe it away, but I need answers. I need to know what she was thinking before anything else happens between us.

"Yes. I am—well *was*—a virgin." She wipes the tear from her eye and takes a deep breath. "Please don't be mad at me. I knew if you knew, you would have stopped it. And I didn't want you to. I wanted it more than you could ever know."

"You're damn right I would have!" I don't want to yell at her, but I can't help it right now. "Annabelle, last night was our first night of figuring things out. We had time. We didn't have to rush it. I could have made it—"

"It was perfect, Jaxson! It was the most perfect night of my life. Please don't ruin this for me!"

Her words come out harshly, but I can feel every ounce of raw emotion leaving her body. Her tears are now heavy, and I can't help it —I go back to the bed and envelop her in my arms.

I know I've made her cry before. I hated myself for it then, but I didn't have to see it.

Now? Seeing this? It's a knife to the fucking heart—one I wasn't sure I had before Annabelle came into my life.

"I really wish you would have told me."

"I didn't know how."

I sigh, knowing that the conversation would have been awkward as hell. Honestly, I don't know how I would have reacted. Now that I'm thinking about it, her being a virgin doesn't surprise me. I knew she was an innocent one, but I didn't realize how innocent.

"Can I ask you a question?"

Her tears have stopped, but her question still comes out strained. She takes my silence as a yes.

"Will you teach me?"

Confused, I ask, "Teach you what?"

She shifts from my grasp so we are now looking at each other. "How to please you?"

I'm stunned by her question. I blink about six times without a response.

"Last night, many firsts happened for me," she says, tracing the tattoo I have with Abigail's name over my heart. "I didn't even know what an orgasm felt like until last night. I know you've been with women—women far more experienced than I am, because, well, everyone is. But I want to please you. I want to give you the pleasure you gave me last night. But I . . . I've never . . ."

I crash my lips to hers, because she doesn't need to say anything else. I might still be pissed at her for not telling me, but knowing that I'm the only man to have ever been inside her? To make her scream? I fucking love that.

And her wanting to learn how to please me and only me? God, I'm getting hard at just the thought.

Last night I made her mine. She's never been with anyone else, and if I have my way, she will never be anyone else's.

Fucking mine.

21

ANNABELLE

"Oh my God! You had sex with him!"

Yup, that's how my best friend greeted me the day after Jaxson and I spent the night, and day, together.

The second Tori saw my face, she knew. I don't know how, but as soon as I stepped into the café that afternoon, she let out a shriek that I'm pretty sure broke glass. She all but ripped off my arm—dragging me back into the office, away from the other workers and customers.

"Oh my God. You did, didn't you? Never mind. I know you did. You've got that just-fucked look going on. It looks good on you. Details! Was he big? Of course he was. Now, lady, I need to know everything."

I just laughed and convinced her to wait until tonight, bribing her with a girl's night to dish all the details. So now it's me, plus Tori's sister Scarlett, at Tori's apartment with pizza and wine.

I had friends growing up, some in college, but I never let anyone get too close to me. My mind was always at home, either wondering if my mom was okay, or after she passed, how my dad was holding up. And even during the few times I did hang out with friends, when they were dishing about who had the biggest dick or who was so horrible in bed they had to fake it, I never participated. I always just hung back, hoping no one would ask me about guys I had been with. I wanted to ask how you would even go about faking an orgasm. Couldn't the guys tell?

Needless to say, it's a bit weird now, sitting here with Tori and Scarlett, as they ask me questions about the best night of my life.

I didn't lie to Jaxson when I told him that it was perfect. I never knew what I was waiting for when it came to my virginity, but now I do. It was him.

After we talked this morning, he was still a bit angry, but he understood where I was coming from. I just had to promise him that as we get to know each other—in and out of the bedroom—if there's anything I haven't done, or want to do, I'll be open and honest with him.

I agreed, but only if he promised to talk to me whenever he was getting too much in his head about us or his past. The hot-and-cold act had to be over.

He agreed, then proceeded to go down on me again. I really liked that.

"All right. Start from the beginning. Don't leave anything out," Tori says as she situates herself on the couch.

"Honestly, when he came to the café, I had no idea what to expect. But then he told me a lot about himself, and his past, which is most of the reason why he's been so closed off with me. Seeing him open up that way? I couldn't stay mad at him, you know?"

I don't tell them about his sister, or the fact that he's been to jail. Some things need to stay private.

Scarlett plops down next to me, two slices on her paper plate. "Yeah, yeah, talking about talking is nice and all, but I want to hear the good stuff. It's been a while for me, so I need to live vicariously through you. Which I never thought I'd say in my life."

"Having a drought? Has Asswipe disappeared again?"

Asswipe is the nickname of Scarlett's baby daddy. Tori has a thing for giving nicknames. I honestly don't even know his name, because Tori only calls him Asswipe. All I know is that he's in and out of the picture, leaving Scarlett to care for their two-year old son pretty much on her own.

Despite the fact that he's here one minute and gone the next, Scarlett can't seem to stay away from him when he's around. She's tried. One time she asked Tori and me to lock her in her apartment all weekend and take her phone, knowing he was coming to town.

"Yes, but I'm done for good with him. I know I'm still going to have to see him because of Grant, but when it comes to him, my legs are closed. For good."

Tori rolls her eyes, knowing it's not the last time we'll hear Scarlett say that.

"Oh, don't roll your eyes at me, Miss Can't Commit. Do we need to ask how many guys you've been out with this month?"

"Nope. You aren't going to turn this on me. We're here to talk about Annabelle and Mr. Dark and Dangerous finally getting it on."

I laugh, the nickname making me smile.

"Honestly, it was amazing."

Both girls sit up straighter, looking at me like I'm telling the most interesting story around the campfire—the smile on my face probably saying everything I need to.

I tell them about our talk at the coffee house, just the important details, and how he took me back to my apartment. I tell them about how he kissed me, and how my first orgasm came on his tongue, which apparently both were shocked about. Apparently, most guys don't like to do that?

"Really?" I ask as both of my friends insist that guys have never gone down on them this early in a relationship. "Jaxson seemed to— well, he seemed to really like it? He did it again this morning."

Tori spits out her wine and Scarlett's jaw drops.

"Is that weird?" I now feel a bit self-conscious.

Tori shakes her head. "Girl, you've got yourself a unicorn."

Scarlett has found her voice. "I swear to God, Annabelle, if you tell me his dick is huge I'm going to hate you forever."

The smile on my face is apparently answer enough.

"Of course he's fucking huge!" Tori says, standing up to pour herself another glass of wine. "Only our virgin friend can find a guy who looks like a fucking Greek god, has a huge dick, and likes eating pussy."

"The most important question is: does he have a brother? Maybe a friend who doesn't mind a single mom?"

I laugh. "I'll have to check on that, Scarlett. Honestly, I don't know that much about his life outside the gym. We're still learning."

Only I know that last word has a double meaning. When I asked Jaxson to teach me how to pleasure him, I had no idea he'd react with such fierceness. He began my crash course right away, showing me how he liked his dick stroked.

I don't know who loved it more: me or him. It was so hard, but had a smoothness to it that I couldn't get enough of. And watching how he reacted made me so hot. Powerful. Feeling his length in my hand, and watching him come apart, made me want to do so many more things with him.

Speaking of which . . .

"So, I have a question for you two, that maybe you could help me with?"

I can't believe I'm about to ask this, but these two are literally the only people I feel comfortable enough asking.

"Jaxson . . . well, he's been with . . ." God, how do I say this? "Well, he's been with many women. He didn't give me a number, but I'm not stupid."

Tori is all but jumping out of her seat in anticipation. Scarlett is smiling like the cat who ate the canary.

"Will you guys—oh shit, I'm just going to say it. I don't know how to give a blowjob and I want to give him one."

I try to mask my embarrassment, but before I know it, my two best friends have come to either side of me, squeezing the life out of me in a group hug.

"I've been waiting for this day for so long," Tori says as she squeezes even harder.

"Our little girl is growing up," Scarlett adds as we all giggle.

"I'm serious, guys." I sit up, breaking the moment. "I've never done anything like that. Luckily, he took the lead on everything last night, but I . . . well, at some point, I want to return the favor."

Tori gets up and sprints to her kitchen. I expect her to come back with the wine bottle, but instead she comes back with a banana.

Oh shit.

The look in my eyes says it all.

"Yup. We're going to practice," Tori says, sitting back next to me.

I eye the banana like it's going to attack me.

"I don't know how to even . . ."

"We'll walk you through it. But keep one thing in mind," Scarlett says, making sure she has my full attention, "the number one rule is: don't bite it."

And for the next hour, my two best friends teach me how to give a blowjob to a banana.

And I only bite it twice.

22

JAXSON

I don't get nervous. Nervousness is weakness. And weakness is how you lose.

I was never nervous for a fight—even the first time I got in the ring with a guy who was four years older than me and had me by 20 pounds.

But now? Getting ready to take Annabelle out for our first official date? Fuck, I'm a wreck.

It's been a little over a week since the first time we were together, but we haven't slept together since. I told her that since I fucked up her first time—even though she insisted I didn't—that the least I could do was take her out on a proper date before we were together again. Or at least our version of a proper date.

Neither of us is the fancy type. Thank God for that. She and I both know that dinner at an upscale restaurant that has multiple forks and foods we can't pronounce would make both of us uncomfortable. So I proposed that we take the day and go for a ride, stop and get food when we feel hungry, and just spend the day together.

And then hopefully the night.

When I pull up to her building and she comes out the door, I have to shake my head, still not believing that this woman wants to be with me.

She's wearing tight jeans that leave nothing to my imagination, and a long-sleeve shirt that is showing off each and every curve. Her hair in a low ponytail is just begging for me to wrap it around my fist later.

If I ever had to picture a perfect woman, she's walking toward me.

"Hey you," she says as she wraps her arms around my waist. In the week we've kept things PG, I've realized that this is her favorite way to greet me. It's my favorite too.

"Hey there." I lift her chin so I can place a light kiss on her lips. It's been a few days since we've seen each other, and I didn't realize until right now just how much I've missed my lips on hers. "You ready to go?"

She nods and puts her small purse in the compartment on the back of the bike. I love the fact that she just does it on her own, and doesn't wait for me to help her. I know this is a small thing, but I also know there are a lot of parts about us that make her uneasy, so any time she takes control and shows confidence makes my heart beat a little faster.

"Where are we going?" she asks as she puts on her helmet.

I climb on, getting situated for her to get on behind me. "I figure we'll just start driving and see where the day takes us."

Her smile is all the answer I need as I put the bike in gear and take off.

We head up Route 41, just riding and taking in the view of Lake Michigan. I've never gone this way, but I thought Annabelle would like the view. And with her arms wrapped around me, practically gluing herself to my back, it's a feeling I won't get tired of soon.

In a few short weeks, her presence in my life has already made me a better man. I feel different. Better. Like I want to make her proud of me.

And to my surprise, I most look forward to the little things. Like when she's at the gym, and she always finds me to give me a kiss hello and goodbye. Or when I stop in for coffee, and make sure that every customer in there knows she's mine before I leave.

We ride for about an hour when I see gray clouds rolling in. Apparently, that small chance of rain was a bunch of crap. Yes, I wanted to impress this girl so much that I checked the fucking weather.

I pull into a diner that's pretty close to Millennium Park, and we hurry inside before the skies open up. We find a booth in the back, and as much as I want to sit next to her, I refuse to be that guy.

I'm not that whipped. Yet.

"I'm sorry. I didn't think it was going to rain today."

She takes my hand in hers, looping her fingers through mine. "It's fine. Plus, I love Millennium Park. Maybe after the rain clears up, we can take a walk?"

"Absolutely. The day is ours. Whatever you want to do."

As we place our orders, the skies open up and a thunderstorm comes down hard and fast. A few of the claps of thunder make Annabelle jump, which is freaking adorable.

We talk about everything and nothing over lunch. I tell her about how I met Kalum and Maverick, and she tells me about Tori and Scarlett. We decide which toppings we'll get when we order our first pizza together, and figure out which favorite movies and TV shows we have in common.

We both know that there are heavier topics we need to discuss, but right now, neither of us wants to ruin the moment.

As I'm paying our bill, the rain comes to a stop, and the sun comes out brighter than it was an hour ago. I don't know why, but this makes Annabelle smile and bounce in her seat.

"Come on! Let's go!"

I don't know what has my girl in such an excited rush, but I'm pretty sure if I don't follow her right now, she'll leave and it'll be hours before she realizes I'm not there.

I take her hand and we walk the short distance to the park. I've been here a handful of times in my life, but visiting the park with Annabelle makes it one of my favorite places.

She finds a spot on some rocks by the water, facing a rainbow that's full of color and light. We take a seat, with her between my legs, and just sit and watch the water hit the shore. She leans her head back against my chest, and honest to God, I can't think of anything better than this moment right here.

"My mom loved rainbows. They were our thing," she says, breaking our comfortable silence. "After every big storm, she would take me to a spot not far from our house so we could paint the rainbows against the skyline."

I kiss the top of her shoulder, loving that she's opening up to me. "That sounds nice."

She sighs, taking my hand, absently playing with my fingers. "It was. Every time I see one, I still think of her. Those are some of my best memories of her."

"Is she—?"

"Yeah. She passed away when I was in college. Cancer."

"I'm so sorry, baby." I squeeze her tighter because I don't know what to do or say. I'm struck by the fact that we've both had a loved one who was taken from us way too soon.

"It's okay. I'm better. Now. But every time I see a rainbow, I just feel closer to her. I know it sounds silly—"

"Not at all. I think it's great."

"Thanks. I sometimes wish, when I see one so bright and beautiful like this, that I had my art supplies with me. I haven't painted a rainbow in so long . . . since . . . well, since she passed."

I turn her around so we're facing each other. "You paint?"

She nods. "Yeah, I actually went to school for it. So did my mom, but she never finished her degree because she got pregnant with me. She made me promise when we found out she was sick to make sure I finished school. Which I did, but since then, I haven't done anything with it. But it was a promise I made to my mom, and I didn't want to let her down."

Thinking back on the little I know of Annabelle, it makes sense. The way her apartment is decorated with so much color—only an artist has an eye like that. And . . .

"The painting on the wall of your apartment—is that yours?"

She nods again. "It was one of my senior projects. It's my favorite. I've had offers from people who want to buy it, but I can't part with it."

"And you shouldn't. Why don't you paint anymore?"

"I just haven't had the inspiration. When I first dreamed of moving to Chicago, it was to open my own gallery. But now, I'm happy with my life. I love the café. It's a good job. Maybe someday the inspiration to start painting again will strike me, but for right now, it's just something I used to do."

And right there, sitting on a rock with a woman who has shifted my world on its side, I make myself a promise that I will do everything in my power to help her find that inspiration again.

ANNABELLE

This day has been absolutely perfect. Even the impromptu thunderstorm.

Spending the day with Jaxson has been nothing short of amazing. After we left Millennium Park, we rode around a bit longer and got dinner at a pizza shop—because after our talk about toppings, we were both craving it. And now we're back in the city.

I didn't want the day to end, and I really hoped he didn't either. It was rare for both of us have an entire day off together, and I wanted to spend every minute with him.

I knew when he didn't drive toward my apartment that he wasn't ready for the day to end either.

We pull up to a building that looks like an old warehouse, but since I see lights coming from different windows, I assume these are now apartments. His apartment.

"I hope you don't mind, but I wanted to show you where I live," he says as we get off the bike and remove our helmets. He says it with a slight hesitation, like I would actually say "no."

"I would love to see where you live."

He takes me up the elevator and we enter a loft-style apartment. It's completely open and it looks bigger because there are just the basics taking up space. It doesn't surprise me one bit that he's a guy who has just the basics to get by.

"This is very you," I say as I look around. "I figured you were a minimalist."

As I look out the window, he comes behind me and puts his arms around me. "I wouldn't say minimalist. I'm just not here much, so what's the point of having a bunch of things? I have what I need. Honestly, it's too big for me, but after where I grew up, I just wanted something more—where I didn't feel like I was living in a shoebox and needed to have six chains on the door."

As we stand there, looking out the window, I revel in the fact that he continues to open up to me. I never press hard with him—I just take the pieces he gives me, and they come a little bit at a time. It's enough, because I know it's more than he has given to anyone else.

I can't help but let out a yawn as we stand in each other's arms. I'm a little tired from the day, but just being wrapped around Jaxson makes me feel relaxed. And safe. I love the feeling.

"You tired, baby?"

Another small yawn escapes. "A little. I didn't realize a day on the bike would wipe me out like this."

He guides me to the couch, where he flips on the TV and positions my feet across his lap. I sink down into the leather sofa, almost falling asleep as he rubs my feet.

"Mmm. That's feels amazing."

Who knew a foot rub could be such a turn-on? Though my body is tired, it's now waking up to the sensation of him hitting certain pressure points.

Whatever he's doing is making my body react. Before I know it, my eyes are closed. I love how it feels when he touches me. My hips are circling, wanting more of anything he'll give.

He stops rubbing my feet, but his hands don't leave my body. They start traveling up, slowly, like he's memorizing every inch. I'm still wearing my jeans, but they are so tight I can feel every touch. He massages my calf before making his way up to my thigh. His powerful hands start kneading into my flesh, and *OH MY GOD, HOW IS A SIMPLE LEG MASSAGE MAKING ME SO WET?*

"Jaxson, that feels so . . . don't stop . . ."

"I couldn't if I wanted to, baby. Just relax and let me explore."

Who am I to argue with that? Every place this man touches me turns me on more than the last.

His hands are now at my stomach, lifting my shirt so he can feel my skin. Like the rest of me, it's hot and ready and waiting for more.

His lips join his hands over my belly button, placing small kisses up higher and higher until my shirt is off, showing my black lace bra.

"Fuck, Annabelle, you are so fucking gorgeous."

His lips continue their journey as he pulls the cups down, exposing my breasts. As soon as they're free, he begins sucking on one, then the other, flicking his tongue against my nipples, which I've discovered is my ultimate turn-on.

My hands are now in his hair, pressing his mouth deeper into my chest. My hips are writhing underneath him, which I can't help. I need a release soon or I'm going to explode.

"Jaxson, I need to come!"

"Not yet, baby. Soon. I'll take you there."

Knowing he will, I let my hands travel down to lift up his shirt. He breaks away from his feast on my breasts for just a second to let me take it off. The feeling of his skin against mine only adds to my want.

He continues his assault on my chest and it's driving me fucking insane. Needing any kind of relief, I position my legs around his hips, digging my feet into his ass, needing him closer so I can find some sort of friction to help with the ache in my core.

This snaps something inside of him, because before I know it, he lifts me off the couch and carries me to his bedroom.

He places me on his king-size bed and we don't need to say anything. The look in our eyes is fire, and we quickly lose the rest of our clothing, needing to feel each other again more than we need our next breath.

He quickly puts on a condom and is on top of me in an instant. Our lips crash together and our hands are everywhere.

He puts a finger inside me—working me, stretching me out, readying me for more. As he adds a second finger inside, I can't help it —my center clenches and my orgasm breaks free.

"AHH! JAXSON!"

Still inside me, he brings me down from the high, but when I look in his eyes, I know we're not done. Not by a long shot.

"Annabelle, do you trust me?"

I nod and my words are soft. "With my life."

Before I know it, he's flipped me on my stomach and lifted my torso so I'm on my hands and knees, facing away from him. Oh my God, is he going to—

"JAXSON!"

He enters me from behind and this is a new sensation. I'm filled in a very different, but very fantastic way. Feeling his thrusts behind me, looking down and seeing my tits bounce back and forth—I love it!

Jaxson takes my ponytail, and with just a little force, pulls me to him. I'm now on my knees, with his chest to my back, and somehow, he's still inside me. He's in control of me, but I know if I say anything, this will stop right away.

But I don't want it to. Ever.

"You are mine. Do you hear that? You. This pussy. You are mine."

"I'm yours, Jaxson. Always yours."

My words are his breaking point. We both come and collapse on the bed with the smell of sex in the air and words that neither of us can take back.

24

JAXSON

I must say, I think I'm getting the hang of this boyfriend thing.

Over the past month, Annabelle and I have nailed down a pretty good routine. I make sure to work nights when she does, so I can ensure she gets home safely. And then, of course, that also means I get to have my fill of her at night.

In fact, there haven't been many nights we've spent apart, which is just fine with me. She might have been a virgin when we met, but not anymore. My girl is insatiable, and pretty willing to try new things. I kind of love it.

And if I'm being real with myself, I kind of love her.

I haven't said those words to her yet. Of course, I know it's way too soon. But for the first time in my life, I have something more than this gym. The best moments are when I put a smile on her face. Like I did the other day when I bought her art supplies: new paints, brushes, and blank canvases. She started crying and launched herself into my arms, peppering me with kisses and showing me how appreciative she was.

That put a smile on my face. And it gave me another idea that I plan to surprise her with later.

"Yo! Earth to Jaxson. You there, buddy?"

Yeah, when I think about my girl, I tend to drift off.

"Sorry, what were you were saying?"

With a smug grin on his face, Kalum leans back in one of my office chairs.

"I take it things are going well with Annabelle?"

It's my turn to smile. "Fucking great, man. She isn't like anyone I've ever met. She's beautiful, and smart, and funny, and so fucking strong and determined. And her painting skills . . . she's amazing. We went to the park the other day and—"

I trail off when I see Kalum looking at me like I've grown a second head.

"What?"

He chuckles. "Nothing, man. I've just never heard you like this before. It's good. I'm happy for you. I'm just wondering when I can meet this woman who has my best friend . . . well, *not* being a moody asshole."

I laugh, because he's right. I don't recognize myself some days, but that's not a bad thing. I'm still not a talker, but at least when members see me around the gym now, I make eye contact with them before giving them a nod.

"Maybe we can meet up for a drink sometime? Bring Maverick. She has a few friends; maybe we can make it a group thing," I tell him.

He smiles and without missing a beat, asks, "Are they hot?"

I roll my eyes. Leave it to Kalum to go there.

"I only know Tori, and yeah, she's easy on the eyes. But be on your best behavior. Last thing I need is Annabelle laying into me because you can't keep your dick in your pants. But you know what? Now that I think of it, Tori might be a little more than you can handle. She's a feisty one."

"Feisty, you say? Yeah, I definitely think we should all go out sometime."

What an asshole.

We shoot the shit a bit longer, figuring out a time when all of us can meet up. Just as we're wrapping up, Reggie comes into the office. I glance at my phone and realize it's about time for him to get out of here, which also means it's mail time.

"All right, Jaxson, here's the delivery for the day. Oh, hey Kalum. Didn't see you there."

The two slap hands as I start going through the stack of papers and mail. Included with the bills and catalogs is an envelope that looks familiar. It looks like the one buried in my desk drawer. And the other one I threw in with it last week.

"What you got there?"

Shit. I must have been holding on to the letter a bit too long, because now Kalum is looking at me and can tell right away something isn't right. He's known me since we were five. He knows my tells, and I know his.

"It's nothing."

"Bullshit. Try again."

I sigh. "Fine. It's a letter from Stan."

"Stan, as in your dad? I thought he was still doing time?" Reggie doesn't know as much about my past as Kalum does, but he does know a little about my dad.

"The one and only," I concede.

"Wait, I saw a letter like that about a month ago. Has he been writing you?" Reggie asks tentatively.

Knowing I won't be able to talk my way out of this one, and that neither of these pricks will give it up, I reluctantly answer.

"Yes, it's actually the third. And a collect call from the prison the other day that I didn't accept. But I'm not opening them. And I won't take his call. Whatever he has to say, I don't want to hear it."

I throw the letter in and slam the drawer shut.

"I'll take that as my cue to go. See you tomorrow. Kalum, good to see you."

Reggie walks away, which leaves Kalum and me staring at each other, knowing neither is likely to break the standoff.

I don't know why he's looking at me like I'm nuts for not opening the letter. He was the one who found me drunk and nearly unconscious after Abigail died. He knew about the fights and the gambling that Stan was fixing.

Out of anyone in this world, he knows why I want nothing to do with Stan.

"Before you say anything, like tell me to go fuck myself, hear me out," he says. "I know your dad is the definition of trash. He should rot in jail the rest of his life for what happened with Abigail. But just so you don't have questions, or make any assumptions, maybe you should op—"

"Go fuck yourself."

I can't believe he'd even suggest it.

"Believe me, I get why you don't want to. If the roles were reversed, I'd probably be doing the same thing you are. I just know that pretty soon, those letters are going to build up and burn a hole through your desk drawer. Maybe it's just easier to rip off the Band-Aid."

He stands up and walks out, knowing there's nothing more to say.

I hate the fact that he's right. The letters have already been on my mind every time I'm in this office. If it were just one, I'd be able to ignore it. But this is the third letter, and the curiosity is almost killing me.

I take the latest letter and shove it in my gym bag. Annabelle wanted to cook me dinner tonight, and I'm not letting Stan ruin a night with my girl.

25

ANNABELLE

"What smells so good in here?"

I can't help but smile as I hear Jaxson coming in the door.

If you would have told me a few months ago that I'd be in Jaxson's apartment, cooking him dinner because he's my boyfriend, I would have told you to go have yourself checked out.

But here I am—in his kitchen, using the appliances I'm pretty sure he's never touched. This whole thing feels very domestic. Normal.

He comes behind me, circles his strong arms around my waist, and places a kiss on his favorite spot on my shoulder. It's downright cliché, but I don't care.

I kind of love it.

Correction: I *absolutely* love it.

And I'm pretty sure I absolutely love him.

I turn around so I can slip my hands around his waist. We see each other nearly every day, but it doesn't make me miss him any less when we're at work.

"How was your day?" His shoulders seem tense, almost like how he stood before we got together. While he hasn't reverted to the shut-off, moody version of Jaxson since we've been together, something feels different tonight. Recently, he's been more relaxed, and it shows in the way he holds his body, but at this moment, he's a little more on edge.

"Fine."

It doesn't matter the gender. "Fine" never means fine.

"Do you want to talk about it?"

Instead of answering me, he nuzzles his nose into my hair, trying to distract me, and maybe himself, from this conversation. It's almost working.

"Baby, you keep doing that and dinner is going to be ruined," I tease.

"Don't care," he mumbles into my neck as he continues to place kisses along my shoulder.

"Well, I do. This is the first time I've cooked for you, and I don't want a horror story that we'll tell for years about how I burned the pork chops," I say as I wriggle out of his hold. He's all but pouting when I free myself. The puppy-dog look on this strong, hot-as-sin man is just too much to handle.

"You, sir, are ridiculous. Dinner will be ready in 20 minutes. And don't think I'm going to let go of whatever is bugging you."

His pouting continues as he leaves the kitchen, placing one more kiss on my cheek before heading to take a shower.

I stopped our nuzzling session just in time, because the pork chops are cooked to perfection. The recipe was one of my mom's that she used to make all the time. She said it was my dad's favorite and that it was the first meal she made him. He always joked that he only married her for the pork chops.

When I said I wanted to cook him dinner, I knew this was what I wanted to make. It made me feel like my mom was closer to me. I so wish I could call her right now to tell her all about the guy who's stealing my heart.

"So, now I ask *you*, what's going through that head of yours?" I didn't even hear Jaxson come back into the kitchen.

"Just thinking about my mom. I do it from time to time when I miss her."

We make our plates and sit at his table. It's not big—just a small table that can sit four—but it's perfect for the two of us.

"What made you think of her today?"

"The pork chops. The recipe is hers. She always made them for my dad—his favorite."

He takes a bite and all but moans as he swallows. God, that was fucking hot.

"I can see why. This is delicious. Thank you for cooking."

"You're welcome. I liked it. Thank you for letting me use your key to get in. Helped to have this all ready so we weren't eating late."

"Speaking of . . ." He takes another bite and then a big breath. "I wanted to ask you something."

What does he want to ask? We were talking about cooking and the key and—

Oh my God, is he asking me to move in with him? I mean, I want to, but I know it's too soon. Tori would slap me. We need to check off a lot more boxes before that can happen.

"What is it?" I take a sip of my water, trying to temper the antic- ipation.

"Actually, let me show you something first."

Since we're almost done eating, it doesn't take us long to finish our plates, at which point he leads me back to one of the extra bedrooms in the loft. It's a three-bedroom space, which is way too much for him. But I know why he got this place, and I know what it means to him.

He opens up a door to the smallest of the bedrooms, and I can't believe what I'm seeing: a canvas and an easel set up by one of the windows, a table full of brushes and paints, and a stool begging to be sat on while art is created.

"What is this?" I ask, knowing but still not being able to wrap my mind around this.

"Your art studio. If you want it to be."

I turn to look at him—his arms shoved into the pockets of his workout pants, looking so nervous but so adorable.

This man, who didn't think that he could be good enough for me, who thought he would hurt me and not protect me, just gave me the greatest gift I've ever received.

"Jaxson, I don't know what to say. Thank you. Oh my God, thank you!" I can't contain my excitement anymore, so I jump into his arms, wrap my legs around his waist, and kiss the hell out of him.

He takes me to the stool and leans on it. I'm now sitting in his lap and getting very naughty ideas of him and me in this space.

"When did you do this?"

He smiles. "Just now, while you were finishing dinner. You had left the supplies here after I'd gotten them for you the other day. Inspiration struck when I was at the gym and I couldn't wait to surprise you."

I lean in and kiss him, showing him how grateful I am for this thoughtful gift.

"I never asked you the question," he says as he breaks his lips from mine.

"You just showed me my own studio space. Whatever you want, the answer is 'yes.'"

He laughs. I love that sound.

"Let me ask it to say I did. I know you miss painting, but your apartment isn't big enough for you to really create the art you want. I have the space, so I set this up. I made you a key, so you can come and go as you please. So, I ask you, Annabelle, would you accept this key? Make some of my space yours?"

I bring my lips to his again. God, this man is everything I could have ever wanted.

"Yes, Jaxson. Thank you. I love it. I love y—."

Oh my God, I almost said "I love you." Shit.

But he noticed, because the smirk on his face says is all. I am completely busted.

"What was it you were going to say?" he says playfully.

"Um . . . I love it. This space. And this stool. It's very good for painting."

He laughs. "Try again, baby, because I'm dying to hear what I think you were about to say. And I think I want to say it too."

I swallow down the lump in my throat. He wouldn't be egging me on if he didn't feel the same way.

"Fine. I love you. I love you, Jaxson Kelly, and I know it's probably too soon and we're still figuring things out, but I love you."

Jaxson's smile is like none I've seen from him before. It's big and bright—such a contrast to the dark and brooding man I'd pined after for so many months. His smile is so big it reaches his eyes—those intense, beautiful brown eyes that I was in love with long before I loved the man they belonged to.

He takes a strand of hair and places it behind my ear. His hand continues the gentle slide from my cheek to my chin, lifting it up to place the softest of kisses on my lips.

"I love you too, Annabelle. So much."

JAXSON

I had a feeling Annabelle would be excited about the art space I made for her. I didn't realize she'd be *so* excited that she would give me a blowjob for the first time in appreciation.

I'll get her 100 art studios if it means getting to see Annabelle with her mouth around my cock. She might still be learning, but she's very eager to please. And she follows directions really, really well.

I didn't lie earlier—I love this girl with everything in me.

We're now in my bed, with her body draped over mine, exhausted from the night. After she went down on me in the studio, I returned the favor. Twice.

"So, what was on your mind earlier?" she says in her quiet tone—the one she uses when she wants to ask me something but is nervous about my reaction. I've told her a thousand times she can ask me anything, but her hesitance is always there.

I don't want to tell her, but I can't lie to her. I promised her I'd be honest. I just never thought I'd have to talk about this ... well ... ever.

"I got a letter in the mail today. Well, I've gotten a few of them recently. From my dad. From prison."

She continues to trace the tattoos on my chest. She loves doing it and I love the feel of her hands on me. And during this conversation, the touches help ease the anger I'm feeling right now toward Stan.

"What did he say?"

"I don't know. I haven't opened any of them."

She stops tracing and rolls off me. We are now facing each other, heads propped up by our arms. I take her free hand, because if I'm going to talk about it, I need her touch to keep me calm.

"Why haven't you opened them?"

I take a breath, trying to figure out the best way to put this, for her and for me.

"I don't care what he has to say. When he went to jail, I was happy. Thrilled even. It might not have been for Abigail's death, but I feel like it was karma catching up with him. He got eight years, and there's about a year left in his sentence. I have a feeling I know what he's going to say, and I just don't want to know. I don't want him in my life, and if I open those letters, I feel like I'm letting him back in."

She releases my hand, only to go back to tracing the ink on my body.

"I won't pretend that I know what it was like for you as a child, or how it felt to lose your sister, and I know your dad was not a good man. He deserved to do that time in prison."

She pauses, and I have a feeling I'm not going to like her next words.

"But everyone deserves a second chance, Jaxson."

"Not him, Annabelle." My tone is much harsher than I want it to be. It's not her fault that my father is scum.

"Just hear me out." She sits up and I follow. This conversation is now turning into something much heavier than pillow talk.

"I'm not saying you have to give him a second chance, but I think you should at least consider it. Open the letters. See what he has to say. You know him, so you'll be able to gauge how you want to act after you've read them. But assumptions are a horrible way to live, and they can lead to regrets. You've made this wonderful life for yourself. You've left your past behind, you have a successful business, and, well, you've made me the happiest I've ever been."

I lean in for a kiss. I know she's not finished, but hearing the pride in her voice was too much for me to handle.

"Be the bigger man, Jaxson. For the first time in your relationship, the ball is in your court. I'm not saying you have to let him back into your life or go pick him up when he's released, but at least open the letters and make the decision for yourself."

She's right. I know she is. And when she puts it like that, it makes a hell of a lot of sense.

Before I can think myself out of it, I get out of bed and retrieve my gym bag from the living room. I didn't realize when I'd stuffed the letter in there earlier that I'd be opening it tonight.

Then again, I didn't think I'd have to tell Annabelle about it either.

I flip on the light when I re-enter the bedroom. Annabelle is sitting up, now with a tank top on. Though I never like to see her clothed in my bed, I'm glad she is. If I don't do this now, I'm never going to do it, and her tits have a way of distracting me.

I sit next to her and stare at the envelope. She puts her arm around me, silently giving me the strength and encouragement I need.

I rip the letter open. The handwriting is familiar, a little shakier than I remember, but familiar all the same.

Jaxson,

This is my third letter, and I'd place money on the fact that you haven't read the other two. I don't blame you, kid. I don't know if I'd read a letter from me either.

But I wanted to let you know that I'm getting out in a few weeks. They're letting me out early. Good behavior and all that.

I know I don't deserve it, and I don't have a right to ask you this, but I'd like to see you. I've had time to think, and I know I did you and your sister wrong. And I'm sorry. I truly am.

I'd like to tell you that in person. Maybe start with a clean slate?

I'll be at your Uncle Stew's place. I hope I hear from you.

Stan

I read the letter over and over and pretty much memorize it.

He's getting out.

He wants to see me.

He wants a second chance.

He's sorry.

It's too much to wrap my head around.

"I don't know." It's all I can say. I don't know what to do. Or what to think.

"You don't have to do anything right now. You have some time to think. But for what it's worth, I think you should hear him out. See what he has to say. Anyone can write meaningful words in a letter. Look him in the eye and judge for yourself."

She's right. I've known Stan long enough to know his tells—to know when he's pulling a con. Well, I learned that one a little too late.

As I lie back down with my girl wrapped in my arms, I know she's right. I need to hear him out.

I just don't know if I want to.

27

ANNABELLE

I knew my life would change once Jaxson and I got together, but I didn't know it would change so much.

And in all the best ways possible.

It's been two weeks since he showed me the space he'd set up for me in his loft, and I've been painting almost every single day. The passion I once had for my art, which had faded after I left college and when my mom died, is back in full force. It's like years of ideas and creativity have been bottled up and are now exploding onto the canvas.

And then the unthinkable happened. I was discovered. Sort of.

I gave Jaxson one of the first pictures I painted. It was fitting considering he's the one who brought my passion back to life. He was so proud of it. It was more of an abstract piece, and he took it to The Pit and hung it up—right at the front where everyone could see it.

Turns out, one of the gym members runs a children's museum and she's been looking for an art teacher. Jaxson couldn't make the introductions quickly enough.

In a whirlwind of events, we went for coffee, she told me about the children's art classes she was looking to begin, and she offered me a job on the spot. I was floored and accepted before I even knew how much it paid.

The answer? Pretty well. So much so that today's my last day at Perks.

It's not the exact dream my mom and I thought of all those years ago, but it's pretty damn close. And I have to think she's smiling down on me right now, beaming with pride.

I'm going to miss this place, but I'm leaving with happy memories. Because I worked here, I met Tori, and in turn met Scarlett. I first saw Jaxson thanks to this place, and strangely enough, if I hadn't walked home alone that night, I don't know if Jaxson and I would be together right now.

Everything happens for a reason. Just like my mom always said.

"You ready to go?" Tori asks as we grab our purses. We both closed the café tonight; it was fitting to do it together on my last shift. "Don't keep me waiting if Jaxson's friends are as hot as he is."

God, I'm going to miss this girl.

"Yes. I'm ready."

With a flick of the switch and a turn of the key, I close the chapter on the place that's been responsible for so much in my life.

To celebrate my new job, and my last night at Perks, Tori, Scarlett, and I are meeting Jaxson, Kalum, and Maverick out for drinks. I've never met them before, though Jaxson has told me a little bit about them. Tori has it in her head that they are, in her words, "fine as fuck."

Like I said, I'm going to miss working with this girl.

Scarlett is waiting for us outside the sports bar, which isn't far from the café and the gym. Jaxson had texted me to say the guys were already inside; they'd snagged a table and didn't want to lose it.

Once we walk in, my eyes find Jaxson's immediately. I'm pretty sure I could be in the middle of Times Square on New Year's Eve and I'd be able to find him.

"Holy shit, Annabelle! You told me he didn't have any hot friends," Scarlett exclaims.

I shake my head as Scarlett and Tori's jaws are nearly hitting the floor at the sight of Kalum and Maverick.

"No, Scarlett, I said I didn't know them."

"Well, I'd like to make it very clear that from this point forward, we are having group outings once a week."

I turn to look at Tori, who has never *not* had a comment when it comes to a good-looking man. But she's speechless.

Hmm, I wonder which one has my friend tongue-tied for the first time ever?

Once we get to the table, we make introductions and the conversation starts flowing. Scarlett and Tori have put their tongues away, and honestly, this is a pretty fun night. I notice that Kalum and Maverick have checked out my friends as well, and my imagination starts running wild to see how all of this is going to play out.

"Okay, folks, now that the small talk portion of the conversation is over, it's time to really get to know each other," Kalum says with a devious look in his eyes.

"Oh fuck. Here we go," Maverick says as he takes a long pull of his beer.

"What's he talking about?" I ask Jaxson, who has kept his arm around me all night. But Kalum answers instead.

"Well, my sweet Annabelle, we need to know more about the woman who has stolen our friend's heart," Kalum says theatrically. "And since you brought two beautiful ladies with you, I feel that we should all get to know each other on a more intimate level."

"Dude, I've told you, no one is going to have a threesome with you," Maverick says as he smacks his brother upside the head.

We all laugh. Kalum is too much. He could give Tori a run for her money in the flirt department.

"No, brother, that's not what I was thinking. I was thinking of a little game called *Never Have I Ever*. Are we all familiar?"

Unfortunately, I am familiar. I played it in college a few times and had to lie my ass off when it came to the sexual questions. For once, I might be able to tell the truth.

"All right, I'll go first," Kalum says. "And remember, you drink if you have done it. Let's see, we'll start simple. Never have I ever . . . had a beer?"

We all laugh at the easy question he tosses up, and of course, everyone takes a drink after clinking our glasses together.

"All right, my turn, buddy. You want to get to know us, let's get to the nitty-gritty," Tori says playfully. "Never have I ever stolen something."

All three guys take a sip of their beer, and so does Scarlett, which comes as a shock to all of us.

"Scarlett! Really?" Tori says, holding her hand to her heart.

"Yes, big sister. It was a dare in high school. And it was a tube of lipstick."

"A rebel. I like it," Kalum jokes.

"Okay, next question," Scarlett says, laughing off the attention. "Never have I ever been arrested."

Again, all three guys take a swig. The girls are clean this round. I really hope we move on from this, but Tori apparently has other ideas.

"C'mon, guys, spill it. We can't have that question and not know what kind of felons we are spending our night with."

I look at Jaxson, nervous about this. He hasn't yet told me why he was in prison. It just hasn't come up, and honestly, it's in the past. I always thought he'd tell me when he was ready.

"Boosting cars," Maverick says.

"Like, stealing them?" Scarlett asks.

"Yup. Lose your keys? We can hot-wire a car in 10 seconds flat. But that life is behind us now. We are upstanding citizens and even pay taxes." Kudos to Kalum for turning the heavy situation into a lighter one.

"I punched a cop," Jaxson says abruptly. Honestly, I'm kind of surprised. I'm sure no one would have pressed if he didn't want to answer.

"Dude, you never told us it was a cop," Kalum says. "No wonder you had to do a year."

Jaxson finishes his beer and continues. "Yeah, I already had two strikes for other stupid fights. Some guy was harassing a girl at some bar. Shit, I don't even remember where I was when it happened. But yeah, I pulled him off her, decked him, then I was the one who got the cuffs slapped on me because the fucker had a badge."

The table falls quiet as I look at Jaxson. As much as I've changed since we got together, I think he's changed even more. Even with revealing just that little nugget of his life, it shows how much he's learning to open up to others. I lean up to press a kiss to his cheek.

"I still love you. I hope you know that."

He turns to me, giving me a kiss that might look PG to the people in the bar, but I know is promising very R-rated things later.

"I didn't want to tell you like that, but thank you."

"For what?"

"For loving me."

28

JAXSON

I can't believe he fucking showed up.

But here he is, standing in front of me.

My dad. Stan.

The reason I don't have a sister.

The reason I'm a fighter.

The reason I am the man I am today.

Yes, I invited my dad to the gym to talk—if I was going to meet him, it had to be on my turf—but for some reason, I didn't think he'd actually show up.

Or rather, I think I was *hoping* he wouldn't show up. And I thought he'd at least give me a heads-up.

"Jaxson. Good to see you, Son."

The feeling is not mutual, but I get up and gesture for him to take a seat. I'm not ready to shake his hand, and we definitely don't have the type of relationship where a hug is called for, but I did invite him, so the least I can do is not be a complete asshole.

He looks exactly how I remember, but so different at the same time. Years in prison haven't been kind to him. He looks older than his 53 years. He's lost weight as well as the little muscle definition he had.

But the confidence is still there. The way he holds himself is how he always made everyone in a room think he was someone special. Or someone not to be messed with. And he still has the same cockiness that paved the way for him to run illegal gambling rings around the city.

"How long you been out?"

"A little over a week," he says as he looks around the office. "You're doing well for yourself. Who knew that me getting you into boxing would lead to this?"

The noise I make comes out somewhere between an exasperated breath and a groan. He says it like he signed me up for Little League and I ended up in the majors.

"Glad to know that you using me for your illegal shit at least worked out for one of us." I can't help but make the dig.

He lets out a sigh and looks straight at me. This is the reason why he's so good at what he does. He can always look a man in the eye, and only the people who have known him for years can tell whether or not he's telling the truth.

But I know his tells. That's why I needed him to come here. I need to look him in the eye when he tells me he wants to make amends.

"Son, I don't want to live in the past."

"No, fuck that. You don't get off that easy. You might have done time, but you and I both know it's not even close to how long you deserved. So before we let this go any farther, I need to know—right now—what you meant when you sent those letters."

No sense in shooting the shit.

"Like I said, I had a lot of time to think, and I wanted to tell you how sorry I am for—"

"For what?" My words cut him off as my anger has now boiled over and I can't contain it. "For getting me mixed into your shit without giving me a say? For using me for your fucking fights? For being the worst husband known to man? For getting my sister—your daughter!—killed? Or just for generally being a horrible human? Because I'll be honest, Stan, I'm having a bit of a problem keeping up with all of the things you need to apologize for."

I've never before unleashed on him like that. After Abigail died, I wouldn't speak to him. Probably because I was afraid I would kill him. Mom had finally divorced him a few years before that, so she didn't like speaking to him most days anyway. But after Abigail died? Hell, I was pretty sure if she saw him, she'd kill him on the spot and then spit on his body.

A few months after Abigail's death, the cops finally got enough on him and he went to jail. I never visited him.

"I deserve that."

"No shit."

We sit in silence for the next few minutes. There's so much to say, yet neither of us wants to be the first to crack.

"I know it doesn't mean anything now, but I want you to know, there's not a day that goes by that I don't think about your sister."

"Me too." That's the one thing we have in common.

"I've changed, Jaxson."

"How do I know that? You've lied to me my whole life. How am I supposed to know when you're finally telling the truth?" It's a fair question. Words only mean so much.

"I know it was my fault."

I nod, though I'm a little stunned by his admission. "I'm glad you can admit that."

I know he didn't attack her, but the men who killed her were after him. Her blood is as much on his hands as the two men who beat her to death.

"I've had a lot of time to think. I know I don't deserve your forgiveness. Hell, I don't know if I'll ever forgive myself. But I've already lost one child and I don't want to lose another."

"You lost me a long time ago."

"That's fair. And I don't expect you to welcome me back with open arms. But I'd like to start fresh. As I said in the letters, clean slate and all that."

He hasn't used any of his tells. No slight twitch in his eye or pulling on his earlobe, which were always his go-tos when he was nervous about a situation. Or so I put together after it was too late.

116

But this is Stan we're talking about—the man I'm pretty sure ran his first gambling ring in preschool. I have a business here that I'm proud of, and Reggie and I have made sure it's stayed clean and on the right side of the law. Do I want him anywhere near my life? This business?

Or near Annabelle?

"I don't know." It's the most honest thing I can say. "I didn't expect you to be here this long. I figured I would have kicked you out five minutes after you walked in. Hell, I didn't even know if you'd show up."

"That's fair. But I'll do anything. Your terms."

I let out a breath. This is a lot to take in.

"I need time to think."

We stand up and he reaches his hand out for mine. I shake my head, not ready for that yet. He nods in understanding.

"I get it, Jaxson. You know where to find me."

"I do."

I figured he'd turn to leave, but the newest addition to my office catches his eye.

"Nice painting. Didn't peg you for an artsy type."

I don't need to turn to know what he's looking at: one of Annabelle's recent pieces.

"I'm not. It's my . . . my girlfriend painted it."

That gets his attention. "You're seeing someone?"

The smile that breaks out on my face is the one I can't control when someone mentions her. Even if it's my deadbeat dad.

"Yeah. And she's the one you need to thank. She's the reason you're here today."

"I'd love to thank her one day."

And like she could sense us talking about her, my Annabelle comes walking into my office with that smile I love so much.

Except Annabelle being in the same room with my father is an unknown I may not be ready for.

29

ANNABELLE

I had no idea what to expect when I was hired to teach at the art gallery. I never saw myself as a teacher. I never even entertained the thought. The dream was always to open my own gallery and share my art with the world.

But as soon as my first student walks into the room, I know I'm exactly where I'm supposed to be.

Since it's still summer, the gallery is filled with classes for all ages. The day flies by in a haze of paints, colors, and ideas. The kids are just as excited for a new teacher as I am to be with them.

When my last student leaves, I sit down and let out the most satisfied breath. I'm covered in paint. My hair probably looks like a rat's nest atop my head. And I've never been happier.

I just survived my first day as an art teacher, and I can't wait to tell Jaxson about it.

I straighten up the room and head for The Pit as quickly as I can. I'm supposed to meet him at the loft tonight, but I can't wait that long. I want to tell him every detail.

Since it's after 5, Reggie is long gone, and the night crew is bustling around, giving classes or talking with members. I'm waving at a few, now feeling like a part of this family, when I hear an unfamiliar voice coming out of Jaxson's office.

"And she's the one you need to thank. She's the reason you're here today."

"I'd love to thank her one day."

Is that his dad?

I knew Jaxson had reached out to him, but I didn't know they had agreed to meet.

I hope it went okay. I know I encouraged Jaxson to reach out to him, but I had no idea how he'd handle seeing him after all this time.

Considering both are still standing and neither is bleeding, I guess it could have gone worse.

I consider stepping back, not wanting to interrupt whatever is going on there, but Jaxson sees me before I can back away.

I give a shy smile and walk in, though I have no idea how to act. This isn't a normal "meet the parents" situation. This is a man Jaxson hates—who has done a lot of horrible things and hurt the ones he supposedly loved.

Jaxson reaches for my hand, knowing I'm out of my comfort zone, and brings me against him. He leans down and kisses my head.

"Stan, this is Annabelle. Annabelle, this is my dad, Stan."

"Pleased to meet you," I say with a hand extended.

He takes it and gives me a firm but not overpowering handshake.

"It's very nice to meet you, Annabelle. I was just admiring this painting. Jaxson said you made it? You are quite good!"

"Thank you," I say, burying myself a little more into Jaxson's side. "I hadn't painted for years, but your son is the reason I started again."

This makes Stan smile. "You're very talented. And you are both lucky to have each other. I'm happy for you, Son."

Sensing the term of endearment is making Jaxson uncomfortable, I quickly try to deflect for him.

"I didn't know you would be here, or I wouldn't have interrupted. I can come back later."

"Stan was just leaving," Jaxson says quickly. I have a feeling he is more than ready for this encounter to be over.

"Yes, I do have to get going. I need to go talk to a guy about getting some work."

Here is where things could get dicey. I know Jaxson was worried about Stan asking for money and was steadfast that he wouldn't give him any. But I don't think he ever considered that Stan would be asking for work.

I look up for Jaxson's reaction. I know that he's looking to hire someone to help around the gym. With the school year starting soon, he's losing a few of his college workers who clean the mats, launder the towels, and do other odds and ends.

But I don't dare offer that up. I have no idea how this meeting went, or if he even wants to see Stan again after today.

"You're actually going to get a real job?" Jaxson asks with a strained laugh. "Sorry, I just never thought I'd see the day."

Stan nods. "Yeah. Now that I'm out, I need to find something. And well . . . not what I used to do. But only so many people are willing to hire a man with a record. I have a buddy who said he's looking to hire someone for some janitorial work. It's not glamorous, but it will get me some money and keep my parole officer happy."

Stan turns to walk out of the office and I nudge Jaxson. I don't want to overstep, but I think this could be really good. For both of them.

"Stan, wait," Jaxson says. "I . . . well, I might have something here. I'm not making any promises, but I can see what our staffing looks like in the next few weeks."

Stan smiles and it looks genuine. If this man is pulling one over on Jaxson, then he's a damn good actor.

"I understand. That would be great. Thanks, Son."

Jaxson lets go of me to walk Stan out. "I'll let you know. Like I said, no promises, but if you don't mind wiping mats and doing laundry, then I could possibly use some help."

He turns and pulls Jaxson in for a hug that makes his son visibly uncomfortable. Reluctantly, Jaxson pats Stan on the back until he lets go.

"Thank you. I appreciate it. Annabelle, it was nice meeting you."

I wave goodbye as Jaxson and I walk back to the office.

"Well, if you offered him a job, it couldn't have gone too badly, right?"

"Neither of us needed a trip to the hospital, so that's a plus."

I reach up and press a kiss to his chin. "I'm proud of you for seeing him. And I'm proud of you for offering him work. I know that couldn't have been easy."

He leans down and places his lips over mine. It's not rushed, but it's also not slow. He needs this kiss, but he's not trying to rip off my clothes. No, this kiss is all about needing each other to be centered again.

Jaxson looks at me thoughtfully and says, "Honestly? I was ready for him to ask me for money or something like that, but the fact that he's actually willing to work for it says a lot. He's never worked an honest day in his life. And he apologized—for a lot, which is also a new thing. He actually admitted Abigail's death was his fault. I didn't know how much I needed to hear that."

"Do you believe him?"

He sighs. "I can't believe I'm about to say this, but I think I actually do."

"Really?" I'm a little shocked by that answer.

He tucks a strand of hair behind my ear before he positions his hands around my waist. "Yeah, I do. I mean, he seemed different. Resigned almost. And that's different for Stan. And considering he spent pretty much my entire life lying to me, I feel like this is the first time he's been honest with me in, well, ever."

I wrap my hands around Jaxson's neck, and gently caress his hairline.

"If your gut is telling you that, then I think you should listen."

He leans down and kisses me again.

"Want to know what I'm listening to right now?" he says as his lips travel to my ear, nibbling on the lobe.

"Hmm?"

"My dick. He's saying that he hasn't seen you in too long and that needs to change. Now."

Well, how could we not listen to that?

We don't even make it back to the loft. I've never been so thankful for a locked door and window blinds.

JAXSON

"Your shot."

I take the cue stick from against the wall and line it up with the striped No. 10. It's an easy enough shot, and honestly, I'm surprised Maverick left it open for me.

I pull back and nudge the ball just enough that it slowly rolls into the side pocket, leaving me a great next shot.

"Thanks, dude. I really appreciate that considering you're solids."

I shake my head. "What? Why the fuck didn't you say something?"

"Because I wanted to see how long it would take you to realize that I would never leave you a shot like that. Then when you didn't, I figured, 'What the hell? Now I only need to make the 8-ball.'"

I grab my beer and take a long pull as Mav easily beats me. I'm usually a pretty decent pool player, but tonight I'm all over the fucking place.

And I don't need a therapy session to know why.

"Dude, what the fuck is up with you tonight? Did you and Annabelle have a fight or something?"

"No, I didn't fucking fight with her."

And thank God. She's the only reason I haven't completely lost my mind since Stan visited me at the gym a few days ago. I have no idea why I even mentioned a possible job to him, but I did. And since then, it's been keeping me up at night.

"Well then, what has you being even more surly than normal? You only get like this when . . . *oh shit.*"

Yeah, Mav knows. He knows that Stan has this effect on me.

"Yup. Dear ol' dad paid me a visit this week."

He goes to get us another round and I grab a table. He comes back with a beer and a shot of whiskey for each of us.

"What's this for?"

He takes the shot glass and we clink before throwing them back.

"Because if we're about to talk about Stan Kelly, then we need more than beer."

He's right. Mav might be a few years younger than Kalum and me, but that doesn't mean he and I aren't close. In fact, there are some conversations I'd rather have with him than Kalum. This is one of them. Where Kalum can be quick to shoot—act now and think later—Maverick is the calm and rational thinker.

"Did Kalum tell you about the letter my dad sent me?"

"Yeah, but I didn't realize you'd made contact with him."

I fill him in on how I got in touch with Stan and how he just showed up at the gym.

"He didn't tell you he was coming? That's kind of fucked up."

"I'm actually glad he didn't. I don't think I expected him to actually show up even though I'd invited him. If he would have, I know I would have figured out a way to cancel. This way, we just ripped off the Band-Aid. But that wasn't even the most surprising thing."

I take a sip of my beer as Mav's eyes almost beg me to get to the bomb I'm about to drop.

"He admitted that Abigail's death was his fault."

Mav nearly chokes on his beer.

"He fucking said that?"

"Yup. After all these years, he finally fucking mans up. I couldn't believe it when he said it. It threw me so hard that I might have offered him a job at The Pit."

The more bombs I drop on Mav, the closer I get to giving him a heart attack. This time, his eyes all but bug out of his head.

"You fucking did *what*? I know I couldn't have heard that correctly."

I stay silent and let him process my words, which is why I'm glad he's the one I'm having this conversation with. Kalum would have punched me by now.

Well, he would have tried to.

"So you offered him a job—"

"Well, technically, I said I might have work for him. Nothing is official yet."

"And now you're wondering whether or not you should follow through with it."

He hit the nail on the head. "Yeah. I mean, words are great, and I wanted to see him in person so I could get a read for myself. But Mav . . . he was different."

"Different how? Remember, this is the man who every time he got out of prison made promises to you, Abigail, and your mom that he never kept."

"I know. Believe me, I remember. But that's the thing. This didn't feel like those times. It didn't feel like the empty promises he used to make. It felt real."

"But?"

"But I've been fooled by him before and I'm not going to fucking fall for it again. I've got a good thing going at The Pit. And I have Annabelle, and if I get her mixed up in—"

Mav grabs my wrist, knowing the road I was about to let my mind go down.

"For starters, you are a grown-ass man who is smarter than the kid you were when he wrapped you up in his shit. Everyone knows you wouldn't have done that willingly. So even if he were in that shit again, you are too smart to get involved in it."

That he's right about. "But what about Annabelle? I can't put her in any danger."

He sighs. Abigail's death hit everyone hard, but Maverick took it especially tough. I think he always had a thing for her when they were kids. But I'd never call him on it.

"Annabelle is a smart and capable woman. But because you're going to make sure that Stan is keeping his nose clean, you'll have nothing to worry about."

"So you think I should give him the job?"

He finishes his beer and stands up. "I think you've already made up your mind. You just needed me to help you talk it out."

He's right. He's 100-fucking-percent right.

"Mav?"

He turns back to me, handing me our abandoned pool cues. "Yeah?"

"Thank you."

It might only be two words, but they're wrapped with a lot of meaning. He knows. We both know.

"Yeah, yeah, now let's play some fucking pool before your woman calls and you go running out of here with your tail tucked between your legs."

I chuckle, rack the balls, and think about what just transpired.

Never in a million years did I think I'd ever speak to my father again, let alone offer him a job. But somehow I feel like this is the right thing to do. And I don't know why, but I feel like Abigail would want me to do this. She was always trying to find the good in people. This would make her happy.

And even in death, I'd do anything for my baby sister.

ANNABELLE

I can feel his tongue between my legs, and damn, even in my dreams Jaxson knows how to elicit pleasure from every inch of my body.

His new favorite thing to do is rapidly flick his tongue against my clit while working two fingers inside me slowly. The combination of varying speeds drives me wild, which in turn drives him insane.

My hands find the top of his head and I hold on to him as he has his way with my pussy. My orgasm is coming fast and hard and—how can I be orgasming from a dream?

Except the clench in my center jolts me awake, and I realize I'm not dreaming. Jaxson was very much having his way with me as I lay sleeping in his bed.

"Jaxson, baby . . . oh God . . . don't stop!"

And he doesn't. He sucks my clit while moving his fingers in and out of me, and soon I'm screaming his name and my legs are shaking with my release.

I open my eyes to see the man of my dreams kissing his way up my body. I knew he was going to have beers with Maverick tonight, but I was feeling inspired to paint. So I used the key he gave me and spent the evening working on a piece I couldn't wait to show him. But I lost track of time and it got to be so late, I decided to stay the night, hoping he wouldn't mind.

Considering how he just woke me up, I'm guessing he didn't mind at all.

"I must say, seeing you in my bed was quite the surprise," he says, continuing his trail of kisses.

"I was painting late into the night and was too tired to go home. I hope you don't mind," I say as I snuggle into his arms.

He kisses the top of my head. "Baby, there's not a night I don't want you next to me or in my arms. You can stay here every night. In fact, I think you should."

Is he asking me what I think he is?

"Jaxson, are you saying what I think you are?"

He rolls me off of him and we lie, facing each other. "Yeah, you're here all the time anyway. Your art studio is set up here. Plus, I would feel much better knowing you were safe here with me. So why not? Move in with me, Annabelle."

God, I want to. The last few months have been more than I could have ever imagined. And if I want to rationalize it, his place is a bit closer to the art gallery than my apartment is.

"Do you think it's too soon?"

"Too soon?" he asks while threading his fingers through mine. "Annabelle, I would have moved you in here the day you gave yourself to me that first time. You make me . . . I'm a better man because of you. You're it for me. Please, move in with me."

I roll on top of him, wanting to be as close to him as possible. At one point, I thought I could never talk to Jaxson. At another point, I thought he'd be too much for me. And now I look at this man who has given me his heart and wants to share his home. How could I say "no"?

I lean down and kiss him with everything I have before I give him his answer.

"Yes, Jaxson. Yes, I will move in with you."

He grabs me again and our lips clash together. This might be the most passionate, intense kiss we've shared, knowing we are about to enter uncharted territory for the both of us.

His hands reach for the bottom of my T-shirt, and we separate only long enough for him to strip it off me. He grabs my ass and rubs my center over his denim-covered cock. The friction is amazing, but I need more.

I need this man inside me.

"Jaxson, I need you."

"Baby, I always need you."

He sits up and I lift his shirt over his head. He flips me so I'm underneath him, and he kisses me one more time before he quickly loses his clothes and rolls on a condom. God, I can't wait until the day I can feel him inside me with nothing between us.

His lips find mine again, and if I didn't need this man inside me more than I needed my next breath, I'd be content. But I need him. I need more.

Reading my thoughts, Jaxson sits us both up on the bed, and my legs instinctively wrap around him.

Never breaking our kiss, he lifts my body just enough to position himself below me, and I easily slide down his length. Our bodies are fused together at every point, and I've never felt closer to him than I do right now.

This is a new position for us, and he feels so deep inside me, I can't take it. I arch my back, which pushes me in even farther as I continue to grind on him. He takes this opportunity to turn his attention to my breasts, sucking on one and then the other so hard he might leave marks.

I don't care. I'm his. He can brand me any way he wants.

He releases a nipple and laps it with his tongue as he brings me back up to him. At first I was just slowly taking him in. Now? I'm riding him like he's a damn bull.

And I love it.

"Baby? Are you up for something new?" he whispers into my ear, sensing that we're both in the mood for something a bit more playful tonight.

"Whatever you want, Jaxson. I'm yours."

He lies back on the bed, making sure he stays inside me the whole time.

"I want you to spin on my dick. Make sure I stay in you, but slowly turn yourself around. Make sure I don't come out. Then when you're facing away from me, ride me like you just were so I can watch your ass as you do it."

The hunger in his voice spurs me on, and I do exactly what he says. I slowly maneuver myself around, so I'm facing away from him now.

"That's it. Now, ride me like you just were. Take what you want from me, because I want you to have it all."

God, this man. His words light a fire under me and I ride his cock like I never have before. We are both so turned on and hungry for each other that this is without a doubt the most intense sex we've had to date. But I do as he asks, and I ride him until I feel my orgasm starting to build in me.

The angle is so different, but I love it just the same. And, obviously, he does too since he's now gripping my hips and guiding me in and out of him, while still letting me control the pace.

I look back over my shoulder and see the fire coming from his eyes, and that's enough for me. I'm done.

"Jaxson!"

"Annabelle. Yes. Now!"

We come together for what seems like forever before I fall face-first onto the bed. Before I know it, he's on top of me, trailing kisses down my back.

"You make me so happy, Annabelle, you don't even know it."

But I do. Because this man is everything I wished for, but never thought I'd get.

JAXSON

There are a lot of uncharted waters for me when it comes to Annabelle.

I'd never been a boyfriend before. I'd never even stayed the night with a woman after sex.

I'd definitely never made an art space for someone or went to a damn farmers' market.

So meeting the father of my now live-in girlfriend is definitely something that could be classified under the "who am I and what the fuck am I doing?" category.

The only thing I know for sure is that I'm making Annabelle happy, and that I'd do just about anything to see that smile I love so much on her face. And when I said I'd go with her to meet her dad, the smile she gave me was worth wearing this button-down shirt.

Yup, Jaxson Kelly—former street fighter and ex-con—is now wearing a button-down shirt and is about to meet his girlfriend's dad. If Kalum saw this, he'd keel over.

I roll up my sleeves as I leave the bedroom to see Annabelle fixing her hair in our bathroom. *Ours.* I know this was the right thing to do, because seeing her in my space, and having her here all the time, doesn't freak me out in the slightest.

I come up behind her and pull her back into me, leaving a kiss on her cheek.

"You look gorgeous."

She smiles at me in the mirror. "You don't look so bad yourself. I didn't know you owned a dress shirt."

I didn't. I might have gone and bought it yesterday. She doesn't need to know that though. And neither does Kalum.

I give her one more kiss on the cheek before I let her go. I love it when she wears dresses, and if I stay behind her too long, we'll be cancelling the trip to see her dad and instead be spending the day with that dress on the floor. She realizes it too, because she finishes up quickly and we make our way to my truck. I don't drive it much, but I didn't want to take the bike today.

I might not know much about meeting fathers, but I know better than to show up for the first meeting on a Harley. And honestly? It's going to be nice spending this time with Annabelle, even if it's just in the cab of my truck for the two-hour drive. Although she's been living with me for a few weeks now, our schedules have been conflicting, so we haven't seen each other as much as we'd like.

"How have your classes been going?"

The mere mention of her students makes her face glow.

"It's going better than I ever imagined." She turns toward me in excitement. "The students are so creative—so much better than I was at their age."

"I doubt that," I say as I link our fingers together. "I'm sure you were amazing."

"I mean, I wasn't bad, but these kids . . . Jaxson, I swear sometimes they're teaching *me* things. But just being able to give them a space and an outlet where they can create their magic and be around other kids who are also creative—it's such an amazing experience. Thank you again for everything."

I kiss her hair as she rests her head on my shoulder. We sit in comfortable silence for a while. It wasn't long ago that I preferred silence because it meant I didn't have to let anyone in. Now it's because I can just enjoy being with someone.

"How are things going at the gym with your dad? I hate that I haven't been able to come in as much as I used to."

"They're actually going pretty well. He's been a real help."

After my talk with Maverick, and of course, after clearing it with Reggie, I brought my dad on board at The Pit. He's done everything we've asked him to. It's a lot of grunt work, but small things like that keep the gym running smoothly and customers happy.

"That's good, isn't it? You sound . . . I don't know . . . surprised?"

"It's because I am. I don't know if he's ever had a legal job in his life until now. And honestly? When I see him around the gym, doing the jobs I've asked him to do, I have to blink a few times to make sure it's him. It's like I don't recognize him. Since he started, he's never missed a shift, he's been getting along with the members, and he and Reggie were even shooting the shit the other day. It's kind of mind-blowing."

Don't get me wrong: just because Stan has been a good employee so far doesn't mean we're going to go out for father-son beers anytime soon. I'm still hesitant, but each day he's proving himself to me a little more.

"Well, I'm glad it's working out. I know it doesn't make up for . . . well, anything that he put you through. But it's good to see he's actually putting in the effort."

As we arrive in Annabelle's hometown, she points out different spots that hold memories for her—the diner her dad eats at every Saturday morning, her high school, and the park where she and her mom would paint.

Before I know it, I'm pulling into the driveway of her childhood home. It's the definition of the suburbs. Thank God I bought this shirt, or I'd stick out like a sore thumb.

I put the truck in park and sit for a second in silence. It hits me how big of a moment this is—for both Annabelle and me.

"Don't worry. He's going to love you."

I look over at my girl, who is looking at me like I hang the moon.

"I've never done this before and I . . . I don't want to mess this up."

She leans in and places a kiss on my cheek.

"You won't. It's not like my dad is waiting at the door with a shotgun."

I let out a breath. I can do this. I used to fight guys who made a living trying to kill people. I can meet her retired bingo-loving father.

"All right. Let's go."

33

ANNABELLE

I did my best to try to calm Jaxson's nerves about meeting my dad, but honestly, I was just as nervous as he was.

I had never brought my ex, Marcus, to meet my dad. It just never felt right, and then when I had finally decided that it was time, well, that was around the time I found out he was cheating on me.

But now that they've been sitting for about an hour in my childhood living room, and the two of them are wrapped up in an in-depth discussion about the greatest boxers of all time, I'm wondering when they're going to realize that I left to get dinner started. The answer is: about 20 minutes ago.

"It's Ali. He's the greatest, and I can't believe you'd even debate it."

I hear Jaxson's frustrated sigh all the way in the kitchen. "Yes, Muhammad Ali is one of the greatest and he's an icon. But how can you take him over Sugar Ray?"

I knew they would get along, but this is going better than I ever expected. I didn't tell Jaxson that my dad and his buddies would get together to watch the fights when they were on cable. I'd hoped that they would discover that about each other and have a bond.

As much as I love them getting along, I can't help but miss my mom a little bit right now. While they would be in the living room talking about how boxing just isn't the same anymore, she and I could be in here sipping wine and getting dinner ready together. She would've loved Jaxson. At least, I hope she would have.

"That boyfriend of yours needs some history lessons," my dad says, startling me. I was so caught up in my daydream that I didn't even hear him come into the kitchen.

I turn to face him and he's wearing a huge smile on his face—a smile I haven't seen much since my mom died. It's nice.

"What?"

"He's a good man, Annabelle. Or at least he seems to be, but I think I'm a pretty good judge of character."

Now it's my turn to smile. "He is, Daddy. He makes me so happy, in so many ways."

When Jaxson turned his spare room into my art studio, I called my dad the next day. I had told him I was seeing someone, but I don't think he knew how serious it was until then. I probably didn't either. Then when I told him about my new job at the gallery, I could hear him smile through the phone.

"Any man who made my daughter find her love of art again and put a smile like that on her face is okay in my book."

He brings me into his side and places a kiss on my forehead while I hug him. I should come back here more often and visit him. We spent so much time together after Mom passed; I'd forgotten how much I got used to him being around every day.

"Do you think Mom would have liked him?"

"Oh, Pumpkin," he squeezes me a little tighter, "your mom would have loved him. The second you told me about him making that space for you to paint again, I knew that was her watching out for you from above. I truly believe she sent him to you."

His words make me tear up. We've never been a very religious family. We attended church a few Sundays throughout the year, so that way we weren't just "holiday-goers" as Mom used to say. But after she passed, my dad and I clung to the fact that she was still with us, in whatever way we needed her to be. In our hearts. In my paintings. In his memories.

Some may call it silly, or say that there's no afterlife. But for us, it's how we coped and grieved. And no one should judge anyone else for how they deal with the loss of a loved one.

I lean up and kiss his cheek. "Okay, no more tears. I have a dinner to finish up and you, sir, need to get out of my kitchen."

He laughs. "You sound exactly like your mom."

He smiles and walks away as a I take the pork chops out of the oven, because since I was coming over here and making dinner, Dad asked for—actually demanded—I make Mom's pork chops.

We sit around the dinner table, chatting like we've done this for years. I don't know what Jaxson was so worried about. I'm pretty sure my dad is about to invite him over in the future, and bringing me might be optional.

"Mmm," my dad says, taking a bite. "Your Mom might haunt my dreams tonight for saying this, but these might be better than hers."

"Annabelle, these are delicious. They're even better than the first time you made them."

"She's made them for you before?" my dad asks.

Jaxson takes a drink before answering. "Actually, the first night she cooked dinner for me was this meal. She said it was your favorite and that her mom always used to make it for you."

My dad nods. "Yup. Only reason I married her was because I realized she'd cook these for me for the rest of my life."

Jaxson chuckles. "I hear you, sir. That's honestly the only reason I'm still with your daughter. She hooked me with the pork chops."

I chuckle and throw my napkin across the table at him. Asshole. He's lucky he's hot.

"None of this 'sir' stuff. Call me Ted."

"Yes, sir. I mean Ted."

My dad takes another bite of his dinner. "Actually, I knew way before the pork chops that I was going to marry Elizabeth."

This takes me by surprise. My dad and I became very close after

Mom passed away, but in all my years, I don't think I've ever heard this story.

"The first time I saw her was at a breakfast joint not far from her college campus," my dad begins. "She was in school, working the counter, and I was just a schmuck who drew the short straw of grabbing the breakfast order for the guys at the factory one day. I was never one of those fancy college guys always coming in and sitting at her counter. I honestly never really had the desire to go to college. I'd gotten a good job at the factory right out of high school and that was all I needed."

He pauses, seemingly reflecting on that time in his life.

"She was the most beautiful girl I had ever laid eyes on, and I knew right there I was going to marry her. She had the most beautiful eyes I had ever seen in my life. I see those eyes every time I look at my Annabelle," he pauses, looking at me lovingly. "But I knew she was a smart, pretty college girl and probably had guys beating down her door. What would she want with a blue-collar guy like me?"

I take a sip of my water, fighting back the tears.

"What did you do?" Jaxson asks.

"Well, I knew she worked on Tuesdays. So every week I convinced the guys on shift to order breakfast, and I always volunteered to pick it up. It took me about five breakfast runs to get up the courage to ask her out."

My eyes lock with Jaxson's. We both feel it: how this story has so many similarities with our own.

"What did she say?" I ask my dad.

"She beat me to it."

I gasp. No way this is about to happen the way I think it is.

"When I was walking over that day, I had my whole speech planned out. And when I got there, I don't know, I just chickened out. Lost all my nerve. But luckily, she didn't, because when I opened up the bag when I got back to the factory, I saw that she had written her phone number on one of the napkins."

I can't fight the tears anymore. And if I'm not mistaken, Jaxson is looking a little teary-eyed himself.

"I take it you called her?" Jaxson asks.

"You bet your ass I did, son. When the woman of your dreams gives you her phone number, you don't throw it away."

I laugh and look at Jaxson as he shakes his head. God, the whole thing feels like it happened so long ago.

"No, sir, you don't," Jaxson says before looking straight at me. "You keep it and treasure it as long as she'll let you."

JAXSON

G od, how long has it been since I've been in the ring?
I used to make sure I sparred with someone once or twice a week. I needed it to let out my thoughts and energy so I didn't do something stupid.

But since Annabelle came along, I haven't felt like I needed it—at least, I haven't mentally needed it. But now that I think about it, I don't remember the last time I went a few rounds.

Considering how I'm gasping for air sparring with Kalum, maybe I need to make a better habit of getting in here a little more often.

"Yes!" Kalum shouts as I place my hands on my knees, trying to suck in air. "For the first time in my life, I've outlasted Jaxson Kelly in a ring. We need a banner. No! We need a party. A big party to celebrate this major milestone in my life."

"Shut the fuck up, you jackass," I say as I step out of the ring.

"I need to thank Annabelle. I knew she was good for you, but her keeping you distracted has benefited me greatly. I need to get her flowers. What does she like? And maybe if I get her flowers, she'll be so thankful that she'll give me Tori's number."

I throw my towel at him as he laughs. He and I have come so far from those days on the South Side. But he's still Kalum, the wannabe ladykiller who doesn't get laid as much as he likes to let people think he does.

"So, I saw Stan here earlier. How's that been going?" Kalum was the most hesitant about me hiring my dad at The Pit. He's not one to forget easily, and he remembers many times when we were growing up when cops would be sniffing around because of things Stan was into.

"As good as it can be, I guess. He comes to work when I schedule him. His parole officer came by last week and said he's been passing all his checks."

"Well, that's something," Kalum says hesitantly. "But remember, man, Stan was always good at hiding shit. You're a smart guy and he had the wool over your eyes for years. I know we were just kids then, but I just . . . I don't want him to fuck you over again. You've come too far."

I nod in appreciation. Kalum's been by my side every step of the way.

"Thanks, man. And believe me, I am being cautious. But I really want to move on with my life, and how can I do that if I'm still holding on to grudges and shit from my past? I want a future with Annabelle, and I don't want what I've been through tainting that. When I propose to—"

"Did I hear the word *propose?*" Stan says as he interrupts the conversation. "Are you thinking about putting a ring on your girl's finger?"

I quickly look around, making sure she didn't slip into the gym without me knowing.

"Yes, though I don't know when. But I've got a ring. I'm just waiting for the right time."

That was another reason I didn't put up too much of a struggle when I agreed to meet her dad. I didn't know when I'd have the chance to see him again, and I wanted to ask his permission to marry his daughter. He of course grilled me about the life I'd provide for her —I respected him even more for that—and in the end he gave me a hug and gave me his blessing.

And her mother's engagement ring.

Now I just have to wait for the right moment. I don't know when it will be, but I know for a fact I want to spend the rest of my life with Annabelle by my side.

"Good for you, Son. I'm proud of you. And Kalum, good to see you, boy. Looks like you've come a long way from the old neighborhood too."

Kalum stands, not reaching for the outstretched hand Stan is offering.

"Yes, I have. I realized a few years ago I didn't want to live a life looking over my shoulder, so I made sure to get my shit straight before it hurt anyone in my family."

We all feel the dig, and I don't blame Kalum. Abigail was like a sister to him too.

Stan hangs his head as Kalum slaps my back and takes off for the locker room.

"I know I deserve everything he just said to me, but it doesn't hurt any less."

I don't know what to say. I might have let him back into the gym, but the cloud of Abigail's death still follows us and probably will for the rest of our lives.

"Anyway, I'm sorry I interrupted you two. I had just come over here to ask you if I could grab your keys. I left mine at your uncle's today and I need to get into the supply closet for a few things."

I agree and he follows me to the office to retrieve my keys. I open the top drawer to get them out, and he spots the ring box I've put in there.

"That it?" he asks.

I didn't want to keep it at home because I knew she'd find it, so I figured here was the best place to keep it.

"Yeah." I open the box and show him. Her mom's ring is simple and classic, just like my girl. I'd offered to pay Ted for it, but he'd scoffed and said that he and his wife talked before she passed, and it was her wish that one day Ted would give her ring to the man who was worthy of Annabelle.

I was speechless.

"I'm happy for you, Son. I really am. That girl of yours is a real sweetheart."

"Yeah, she is."

"Listen. Get out of here. There aren't too many people left tonight. Go surprise your girl. I'll lock up."

It's my night to shut down the gym, but he's right, there are only a few people left, and it looks like they're wrapping up their sessions soon. And I would love to surprise Annabelle at the gallery.

I hesitate though, because leaving my keys with Stan gives me pause. I had only given him a key to the storage rooms. He still has a long way to go to earn back my trust, and giving him the keys to The Pit is a big step. Even if it's just for a night.

"I know what's going through your head."

"Are you going to say it, or am I?"

"You're thinking to yourself that I shouldn't give my ex-con of a dad who used to run illegal fights the keys to a gym that has more fighting equipment than a sporting goods store."

Well, he hit the nail on the fucking head.

"I'm going to be honest with you, that's exactly what I was thinking. Things have been going well, but this is a big step and I'm not sure if I'm there yet."

He nods in understanding.

"I get it, Jaxson. Hell, I don't know what I would do if I were in your shoes. But it's just one night. Let me prove to you that I've changed."

He's looking me dead in the eyes and doesn't even flinch. Not one eye twitch.

"Don't make me regret this."

He smiles at me like the time I won my first boxing match.

"I won't, Son. You have my word."

35

ANNABELLE

"All right, ladies. Lastly, we're going to paint the words you chose to use on your signs. I'd recommend a bright color, like a white or a yellow, but customize it with whatever color is calling to you."

"Is someone calling for more wine? Because I seem to be empty," one of the women in my class says, slurring her words a little.

I just laugh, grab another bottle, and set it on her table. While I love teaching the kids during the day—my aspiring artists of the future—teaching these pop-up paint-and-sip nights are fun. Here is a group of women who want to get out of the house and have a night for themselves, while making something they can hang in their home. It reminds me that not all art has to be sold in a gallery; it's just something that can give you joy and an escape for a few hours.

It helps that I sip some wine as well.

I walk around the room, glancing over shoulders just to make sure no one is ruining their projects.

"Why does mine look nothing like the example you have?" Tori huffs in defeat. When I told her about these classes, and that wine was involved, she and Scarlett invited themselves to come. I didn't mind, though, and since this was a pop-up, they blended right in.

"Probably because you've just downed an entire bottle of wine all by yourself, and you couldn't even color inside the lines in kindergarten," Scarlett goads her.

"Hey! I was told that I was too creative to stay in the lines!"

"Oh dear, Sister. They lied to you. I'm sorry you're just now realizing this. Also, Santa isn't real."

Tori throws down her paintbrush.

"Well, dammit! Here I thought I was special."

"Oh, you're special all right." We all just laugh. Now that I'm with Jaxson, I haven't seen them as much as I used to, but the nights we do get to spend together are just like old times.

I continue to walk around the room as the women finish up their new welcome signs when one of them calls me over to ask my advice on colors.

"Oh my God. Who in the hell is that man walking in?" one of the women next to her says.

"I don't know, but whoever he's here for, I'll be her for as long as he wants me."

I look up and smile as I see Jaxson walking into the gallery with a bouquet of flowers. He hasn't shaved for a few days, and the scruff on his face makes him look even sexier than usual. Pair that with the tight T-shirt that's showing off his tattoos and he's every bad boy fantasy come to life.

"Okay, ladies, we have about 10 more minutes, so put the finishing touches on your projects."

I walk over to him and I hear every woman except Tori and Scarlett giggle and almost swoon over my man. I could be jealous. I could tell them to back off and that he's mine. But all I do is smile and laugh, because I know he's not looking at a single one of them. His eyes are locked with mine.

"What are you doing here?" I reach up and wrap my hands around his neck, giving him a light kiss. "I thought you had to close at The Pit tonight."

He picks me up—just enough to lift my feet off the ground—so he can kiss me a little harder. Nothing inappropriate, maybe just a little PG-13.

"Actually, Stan is locking up for me tonight."

He sees my look of confusion as he puts me down. I knew things were going well, but that's a big step in the trust department.

"Really? I mean, if you're comfortable with that, then it's great. But I didn't know you two had reached that place yet."

He rubs a hand over his short hair and all I can think about is that I want to do that too. Tonight. While his face is between my legs.

"He's been doing well, and there was only about an hour left before we had to lock up anyway. I only gave him the key for the door. We're not at the level where I'm about to trust him with money yet."

I grab his hand and lead him to the back of the room as the class finishes up. The catcalls calmed down after they realized he was with me. It doesn't stop the gawking though.

I get it, ladies. I really do.

"So, are those flowers for our girl or do you just crash girls' nights to give a random lucky gal a bouquet of flowers?" Tori teases, which makes Jaxson laugh. I love that these two get along so well.

"No, these are for Annabelle," he turns and gives me the gorgeous bouquet of stargazer lilies. "Though Kalum *did* say he was going to buy Annabelle flowers because he bested me tonight in the ring; he thinks it's because she's been keeping me occupied."

I laugh, though it's probably true.

"Actually, Tori, Kalum did say that he should ask Annabelle for your phone number."

Tori rolls her eyes and I can't stop laughing now. The few times Tori and Kalum have hung out with us, it's been quite the sight to behold. They are both shameless flirts and quick to the trigger. Anyone in the room with them can see that they have the hots for each other, but both are too hardheaded to make the first move.

"You can tell Kalum that he can grow a pair and ask me himself," she says as she picks up her purse and her *Home is where the wine is* sign that she painted tonight. "Then I can be the one to tell him I wouldn't fuck him with someone else's vagina."

Jaxson keels over in laughter and Scarlett and I are now crying. One day, this girl is going to find her filter. But then again, she'll probably be the old lady who gets kicked out of the nursing home for being inappropriate.

"Oh, Tori," Jaxson says as he collects himself, "please make sure I'm there when you tell him. And that my phone is charged. I'll need to take some video so he can watch that every day for the rest of his life."

We make sure that everyone is gone, and Jaxson and I lock up the gallery. It's a beautiful night. The weather hasn't taken a turn to fall quite yet, so we take advantage and walk the few blocks back to the loft, picking up a pizza on the way.

"I've been thinking lately," Jaxson says, breaking our comfortable silence.

"About what?"

"The first time I saw you. I've been thinking about it a lot since we went to your dad's for dinner."

If it's the same day I first saw him, I'd rather he have a different memory.

"Please don't tell me you remember me for nearly spilling coffee on you only to knock over a display of gift cards instead. Because I'd rather that not be the story we tell our grandkids someday."

I stop myself. I don't know what made me say that. We've never really talked about kids. We've joked a few times about marriage, but nothing concrete.

Of course I've thought about it. A lot. A little baby Jaxson causing trouble, but secretly being a mama's boy, and a little girl with my red hair worshipping the ground her daddy walks on. The two of them running around The Pit, getting into anything and everything.

He stops and takes my hand in his, looking at me with all the love in the world—with those deep brown eyes that once held only pain and anger behind them.

"No, I'm going to tell them about how when I saw their mom, her beauty rendered me speechless for months. And that though I didn't know it at the time, she saved my life."

I don't care that we're on a sidewalk in Chicago—me holding a bouquet of flowers and him holding a deep dish pizza. I kiss him with all that I have, and everything I want to give him.

Because he saved me too. In so many ways.

JAXSON

I look at my phone and see that it's 4:30 in the afternoon, and although I'd like to take a lap around The Pit to see how everything is going today, I know Reggie is about to come in with his daily mail call.

But when he walks in, he doesn't have a stack of papers in his arms. Instead, it's just his coat and satchel.

"Do I actually not have homework tonight?" I joke. "If so, this might be the first time since we opened that you haven't given me things to do when you leave. Go before you change your mind!"

"Actually, I wanted to talk to you about something, but I'd rather not do it here," he says, almost nervously. "Do you think we could talk somewhere else?"

"Yeah. Is everything okay?" I ask as I grab my keys and jacket.

"I hope so. I'd just . . . I'd just rather talk in private."

We head to my loft since Annabelle is at the gallery. I grab us a few beers and we take a seat around the island.

"Dude, I gotta say, this is kind of freaking me out. What's going on that we couldn't close the door and talk about at the gym?"

Reggie runs a hand through his hair and takes a long pull of his beer. "Honestly? I don't know yet, but I'm noticing some weird things and I wanted to bring them to your attention, but I didn't want anyone to overhear because it could be nothing."

"Or it could be something," I say, finishing his thought.

"Yeah, it could be."

Reggie begins explaining that it started with the security camera in the alley getting broken again. He didn't tell me because he honestly thought it was the same punk kids who did it the first time, and it wasn't too much of an expense to replace it since we've doubled our membership.

"If it had just been that, I honestly wouldn't have thought anything of it. But Jaxson, money has been going missing."

This takes me by surprise. Reggie is meticulous about our books—down to the last cent.

"How much?"

"Every day we're missing anywhere from $50 to $300. It's never the same amount."

In the time since Reggie and I opened The Pit, we've never had trouble with any employees or theft. This just doesn't make any sense.

"How long has this been going on?"

He gives me a sobering look. "It started a few weeks after your dad came on board."

I shake my head, though I really don't blame him for thinking it.

"No, it couldn't be him. He doesn't have a key to the safe or the lockbox. Stan Kelly is many things, but a thief isn't in his repertoire." One time, back when I was a kid, we were locked out of the apartment and he couldn't even pick a 20-year-old lock to get us in. Instead I called Maverick, who could pick a lock by the age of five.

"I have no proof it is or isn't him, Jaxson. I just know that that's when money started going missing. I don't know how you want to handle this, but I figured I needed to talk to you about it sooner rather than later."

I thought about all the times my dad would have had the opportunity to swipe from the box or the register, and honestly, there haven't been many. He closed The Pit that one night I surprised Annabelle at the gallery, but since then, he hasn't closed without someone else there. There are too many people around during the day who would've noticed him stealing money, and the petty cash is locked in my office every night.

While he's rightfully the top suspect, it just doesn't add up. There's something missing.

But I know a surefire way to find out if he's the one behind the missing money or not.

"Grab your jacket. Come back to the gym with me. I have to see something before we decide anything else."

I don't tell Reggie what we're about to do, because I don't even want to tell myself.

As soon as we get back to The Pit, I run to the office and unlock my top drawer. I'm the only one who has a key, but if someone is figuring out how to get into the safe, then this drawer would be child's play.

When I open the drawer, my stomach drops like I'm on a roller coaster. Inside I find only paperwork, a few paper clips, and an assortment of pens.

The engagement ring is gone.

"Fuck!" I yell, standing up and punching the wall.

"What?" Reggie is confused. "What was supposed to be there?"

I pull at my short hair, wishing it were longer just so I'd have something to rip out right now. How could I be so fucking dumb?

"I . . . Annabelle's dad gave me her mother's engagement ring. I locked it in the desk so she wouldn't find it in a drawer at the loft. Stan was the only one who knew it was in there."

I knew I should have listened to the voice in the back of my head that said to proceed with caution—that at the end of the day, he was still Stan Kelly, career criminal and general piece of shit.

But now I'm left wondering how the fuck I got into this mess.

ANNABELLE

When I caught Marcus cheating on me, I had a weird feeling that day that something was off.

It's the same feeling I've been having with Jaxson.

It's been two days since we've seen each other. That isn't completely abnormal for us, but normally when our days don't sync up and I'm in bed before he gets home, he wakes me up and kisses me goodnight.

But the last two nights he hasn't. And last night he slept on the couch. Tonight he's home for dinner, but he might as well be a million miles away.

I'm trying not to freak out. But damn, it's hard not to let my mind think the worst.

Did something happen with his dad?

Maybe he regrets asking me to move in?

Is he seeing someone else?

"Is everything okay?" I ask him.

"Yup."

Well, isn't that an enlightened answer?

"Is something wrong with your chicken?"

"Nope."

"Then why are you picking at it like a child who doesn't want to eat his broccoli?"

He slams his fork down. "Why do you care so much about how I eat my dinner?"

Like hell he's going to snap at me when he's the one acting like an ass. "If it were just about your dinner, I wouldn't give a damn! Maybe it's because you voluntarily slept on the couch last night and I haven't seen you in days! Why is that?"

"I'm sorry I didn't want to wake you up. God, I'm such a horrible person for letting you sleep. Call the police on me."

"You didn't mind waking me up last week with your tongue. Or do you only wake me up when you want to fuck me?"

"Now I'm an asshole for eating your pussy? Sorry it was such an inconvenience for you."

That's it. We're both pissed off and this is going nowhere. I'm not going to argue about random shit just because he's too hardheaded to tell me what's actually bothering him.

"I don't know why you're being an ass, but I'm not going to sit here and take it. You are obviously in your head about something. And you promised me that when something like this happened, you would come to me. That we would talk it through. So here I am, asking you to confide in me."

He doesn't look at me, doesn't speak, just continues to push the chicken around his plate.

"Fine," I say, grabbing my plate and dropping it in the sink. "I'm going to bed. Since you seem to be quite familiar with the couch, you can stay there again tonight if you aren't going to tell me what's wrong."

I charge off to our bedroom and slam the door shut.

As soon as I hit the bed, my tears fall. I've always been an emotional person, and I can't believe my angry tears didn't come during our epic yelling match. I'm surprised our neighbors didn't call the cops on us.

He promised me he wouldn't do this—that he wouldn't go back to the Jaxson who would refuse to talk to me when things got hard. And he *had* been better. These last few months have been the best of my life. I thought they were for him too.

Maybe the honeymoon is over? God, I hope not. I might be angry with him, but he's the love of my life. I know that as much as I know anything.

I don't hear the door open, but I feel his weight as soon as he sits on the edge of the bed. My head is buried in the pillow, trying to muffle the sound of my crying.

"I hate it when you cry," he says, his voice strained.

I roll over and sit up, wiping the tears as best I can. "I hate it when you make me cry."

His hand reaches out for my leg, and his touch starts to calm me. He massages it gently, and I know he's trying to find his words. This I can work with. This is better than screaming at the dinner table.

"What's the matter, Jaxson? I thought everything was going well, and that we were fine, but the last few days you've been so . . . gone."

He doesn't answer for a minute, and with every second that passes by, my nervousness grows a little bit more.

"Annabelle, I don't know how to say this . . ."

Oh God. Is he breaking up with me?

"Stop. Don't say it." I have to cut him off. I don't want to hear the rest.

"Say what?" he asks in confusion.

"If you're breaking up with me, I don't want to hear the words. I can't hear them. I—."

Before I can finish the thought, he makes his way to me, crashing my lips with his. I've missed his lips so much. How he claims me a little more each time our lips join.

This kiss is intense and consuming and there is no way he'd be kissing me like this if he were leaving me. That's my only solace right now. So I give back just as much as he's giving to me.

"I can't believe you'd even think I would be ending this," he says, now on top of me. "Don't you know how much I love you, Annabelle? That I would die for you?"

I wrap myself around him, needing to feel connected to him as much as possible.

"I love you too. But when you didn't sleep in our bed last night, my mind just took off in a thousand directions."

He kisses me again, not as forceful this time, but there's something different about this kiss than the hundreds we've shared before. He's now covering me with his body and his weight is nearly crushing me, but I don't care. He chose to spend the last two nights away from me, physically and emotionally, and right now I need to feel him.

His lips are everywhere as he tries to remove my clothing without breaking away. It's next to impossible, but he doesn't seem to care. It's like I might disappear if he moves even an inch from me.

He makes his way back up my body, placing kisses over my breasts, along my neck, on my ear, across my cheek, and then finally on my lips.

"I'm so sorry I worried you. I'm sorry I was the reason for your tears. Again. Please know that I love you. I love you so much, Annabelle."

He slowly removes my clothing while tracing his hands over my body. It's like he's trying to memorize every curve.

"I don't deserve you. I never have. You are perfection."

I sit up on my knees, mirroring his stance, and wrap my arms around my neck.

"We are perfect. Together."

No more words are spoken. We spend the evening making love—taking it slow and savoring every moment.

I realize he hasn't told me what's wrong, or why he's been acting the way he has. And maybe I should have pushed harder for an answer.

But he's back with me. At least for now. And that's all I need.

JAXSON

I didn't sleep a fucking wink last night. Luckily, Annabelle fell asleep in my arms, so she didn't realize all I did was stare at the ceiling.

How the fuck did I get myself into this situation?

How was I so fucking blind that I didn't realize Stan was back to his old ways?

Those are just a few of the questions I've been raking over in my mind since last night. Luckily, Stan is off today at The Pit, so I have time to figure out my next steps before confronting him. Or punching his face in. That will probably happen no matter when I see him next.

My body and mind are tired, and I can't focus, so I grab my gloves and decide to go a few rounds with the speed bag. It's pretty late. We're open, but it's a Friday night and no one is here, so I appreciate the peace. Just me, the bag, and the mountain of problems I all of a sudden need to face.

If he were only stealing a few hundred dollars, he wouldn't be in that deep. And the ring has more sentimental value than anything else. It has a smaller diamond in it, but I knew Annabelle would love it more than any high-priced ring I could get her.

Without a doubt, I'm firing Stan tomorrow. That's a fucking fact. He knew he had one chance with me, and he blew it.

I know gambling is an addiction, and I feel for the people who truly suffer, but with Stan, I don't think it *is* an addiction. It's his life. It's the only life he knows.

And again, he chose that over his family.

My fists are connecting with the bag at a rapid-fire pace, and the only sounds in the gym are the bag hitting the platform and my breaths growing heavy. That is, until I hear the front doors open and see two dudes—so big they make me look tiny—come around the corner.

I don't know them, but I know exactly why they're here. Two guys who look like that—with their imposing frames, slicked-back hair, and tailored suits—are absolutely the kind of guys Stan used to run around with when he was setting up his fights.

Seeing these guys makes my stomach tighten, because I have a feeling that dear ol' dad is in a lot deeper than a few thousand bucks.

"Gentlemen, what can I help you with?" I step away from the bag, but don't take off the gloves.

"Where's Stan?" one of them says.

"Not here. Who wants to know?"

"We're friends of his. We need to pay him a little visit."

"Why did you think he was here?"

"He can't stop bragging about this place. Your pops is real proud of you, Jaxson."

The drop of my name is on purpose—his way of telling me he has the upper hand here. I might not remember him from back in the day, but this isn't my first rodeo.

I can play this one of two ways. I can act dumb. See what they'll tell me and hopefully it's enough to figure out the depth of the shit Stan is in—or more specifically, how deep I'm in it.

Or I could play along and see how much information they'll drop.

Considering I don't know if they're packing, and I don't want to say the wrong thing that could land me a trip to the hospital, I go with the first option.

"Well, he's not here. Haven't seen him today. But I'd be happy to tell him you guys swung by. What did you say your names were again?"

The smaller of the two, the only one who has been saying anything, speaks up again. "We didn't say who we were. We know where to find him. We were just hoping to talk to him a bit in private. It's in good taste to try to collect 200 large without company around, if you know what I mean."

"I get it." How I said that with a straight face, I'll never know.

Two hundred fucking thousand dollars? He's only been out for two months! How in the actual fuck do you get 200 grand in the hole that quickly?

But I have to keep my cool. The only way I'll get any info is if I play along.

"Well, I'm just about ready to shut down for the night, so if you don't mind . . ." I don't finish the sentence, hoping they aren't going to put up a fight and demand something from me.

"Actually, we do mind. Because you see, Stan told us all about you —that you're a pretty good fighter."

I shake my head. "No, man. I used to fight, but those days are long behind me."

The smaller guy takes a step toward me. "I don't know. I saw you with that bag. It looks like you still have some gas in the tank. You think about getting back in the game? Or does your girl not like you fighting?"

I want to throttle this guy because now he's just pissing me off, and he's slyly let it drop that he knows I'm with Annabelle. But I can't react to this, even though I want to kick his ass for even breathing a word about her.

"No, man. That life is long over. Those young kids would wipe the floor with me. Plus, the police cracked down hard on the fights a few years back, didn't they? I didn't even think those existed anymore."

Take the bait you dumb fucker . . .

"We find our ways," he says with a gruff laugh. "If you ever want to get back in, tell Stan to get in touch with me. He knows how. You could sure bring in a pretty penny. People would line up around the block to see Jaxson Kelly fight again."

"Thanks, but I'll pass."

"Suit yourself, kid." The two walk past me, but instead of turning around to leave out the front door, they head to the back door, which leads to the alley. The alley that's had the security camera fucked with. The alley that no one uses other than employees.

Their visit, and exit, raises every warning bell in my brain. Instead of going back to the loft, I sit in a dark part of the alley and wait, hoping I don't see what I think I'm about to.

But instead, I see exactly what I was afraid of.

Stan at the back door. A goon with him. Other people arriving, being ushered in a few at a time.

I know this crowd. Not these specific people, but I know the type. I know the routine.

Stan Kelly is running fights out of my gym.

I want to say I can't believe it, but I can.

How big of a fucking idiot was I to give him just the little bit of access into my life he needed to make this happen?

How could I not see this coming?

Seeing all I need to see for the night, I jump on my bike and just start riding, thoughts swirling through my head.

First and foremost, I have to come up with a plan. To get my money back. To get Stan out of my life. To shut down the illegal fights going on in my gym that would send me back to jail in no time. To get the thugs who would ruin me in a second away from my life—thugs who would hurt Annabelle without thinking twice.

Just thinking about that last part makes me physically ill, because she's the love of my life. I know I'll never find anyone like her, and I have to make sure she's safe. I have to make sure they don't bring her into this shit.

I have to make sure she stays alive.

I have to tell Annabelle goodbye.

ANNABELLE

When he didn't come home the first night, I didn't realize it until morning. I told myself that he must've had an early day and didn't want to wake me up.

When he didn't come home the second night, I knew in my heart something was wrong, but I didn't want to alarm anyone. But I stayed up all night, waiting for him to come through the door.

He never did.

It's now been more than 72 hours since I've seen or heard from Jaxson, and I'm experiencing a full-on panic attack.

I went to The Pit to see if Reggie had heard from him. He had earlier yesterday—a vague text saying he had to take care of some things and that he'd be gone for a few days. Reggie had assured me that Jaxson was fine and that I shouldn't worry.

Yeah right.

I'm part-relieved that he's alive and part-pissed that he would text Reggie and not me.

How could he do this to me? He promised he wouldn't ghost me like this. Or at least he promised that before last week, when he started to grow distant.

But wasn't it just a few days ago he was telling me he loved me and that he didn't deserve me? Now I don't even get a text message telling me whether or not he's alive or dead in a ditch.

God, I'm so fucking confused. I knew I should have pushed harder the other night. But then again, maybe he didn't want me to, and that was his way of telling me goodbye.

I'm pacing the apartment when I hear a knock on the door.

Before I can answer, the cavalry lets itself in. Not only are Tori and Scarlett here, whom I had messaged to come over earlier, but on their heels are Kalum and Maverick.

"What are you guys doing here?" I was so in my head I didn't even think of trying to get in touch with the two of them.

"Tori called me after you texted her to see if I had heard from him. Which I haven't. That asshole. Why didn't you call me?" Kalum asks.

I'm going to ignore the fact that Tori has Kalum's number. I'll save that for another day.

"I . . . I don't know. I should have. I'm sorry. I just can't think. I don't know what to think."

Maverick comes over and puts his arm around me, bringing me to his side. "We'll find him, but we need to figure out where the hell he could be first."

Apparently finding a missing person requires pizza and beer, which I'm thankful for. I haven't eaten since, well, I don't remember the last time. And the beer might not be the best idea on an empty stomach, but hopefully it will calm my nerves.

I fill them in on the last night I saw him. Well, not *everything*—just the important stuff. And I recount the few days before that, when he had seemed distant.

"And you're sure that Reggie talked to him?" Tori asks.

"Yeah. He didn't show me the text or anything, but I believe him. Reggie is a good guy and his business partner. If Jaxson had truly disappeared without a trace, I'm pretty sure Reggie wouldn't have lied to me."

"Let me call Reggie and see what I can get out of him," Kalum says and steps into the hallway to make the call.

"Mav, you and your brother know him better than anyone else. Do you have any idea where he'd go?" I plead.

Maverick runs his hand through his hair, clearly frustrated by our lack of information. "I honestly don't know. He might have stopped at his mom's, but there's no way he would have camped out on the South Side for three days. Too many memories. He rarely gets out of the city, and if he does, it's nothing more than a day trip. I'm so sorry, Annabelle. I wish I could help more."

Scarlett moves to sit next to me on the couch, bringing me in for a hug. "We'll find him. Then we'll kill him. But I promise you we *will* find him."

"Apparently, we need to find Stan, and then we'll find Jaxson," Kalum announces as he walks back in.

Stan? This has to do with his dad?

"What did Reggie say?" I need to know. I need to know *something*. Anything.

"He didn't know much. Apparently, some money had gone missing from the gym, and Jaxson and Reggie figured out Stan was stealing it. My guess? Jaxson went to confront him and get his money back."

That makes sense, though I don't understand why that would warrant not telling me that he's still alive. Something isn't right, but at least we know more now than we did 20 minutes ago.

"I think I heard Jaxson say that his dad was staying with his brother, Jaxson's uncle, but I don't know where that is." While my anger is growing with Jaxson, I feel horrible for him. He let Stan back into his life, and he used him again. I hate that I feel like I pushed him to try again, only to be let down one more time by his own flesh and blood.

"His uncle is in the old neighborhood," Kalum says. "We'll go check it out, but if Jaxson found him, I doubt he'd still be there."

Tori is in a huff. "So where would he be? It's been days. *Days*, Kalum! How the hell could he just fucking leave her?"

While I love Tori, her words hit me hard. Because she's right.

How could he just leave?

What if he doesn't come back?

Or worse, what if he does, and he retreats to the old Jaxson for good? The one who wouldn't let me in?

That Jaxson would leave me. And now that I've been with him, I can't imagine my life without him.

My tears are threatening again, and I don't want to fight them anymore. I just want to turn back the clock to last week when I was in Jaxson's arms, thinking I had found my future.

"What do we do?" It's the only question I can think to ask.

The room is silent for a minute—no one really knowing what the answer is.

"You girls stay here, and maybe the asshole will come back. Maverick and I will go snoop around the old neighborhood. Maybe someone saw something."

The guys stand up to leave, and Tori walks them out. I can't move. I'm paralyzed. My head is in a million places and it's too much to process.

It takes me hours to finally fall asleep, but my exhaustion takes over around three in the morning as my dreams are haunted by brown eyes and tattoos.

40

JAXSON

That fucking sleazeball.

I look at Stan, perched up against the bar at this dive like he doesn't have a care in the fucking world. Like he's not a fucking criminal in the hole $200,000 to wannabe mobsters.

I'm going to fucking kill him.

When I drove away from The Pit after figuring out that it was being used for Stan's fights, I just kept riding around Chicago until the sun came up. I eventually ended up at Millennium Park and the same rocks Annabelle and I sat on during our first date.

As I watched the sun come up, everything became so much clearer to me.

When it comes to Annabelle, I've been living a lie these last few months. How did I think that I was actually worthy of her? That my past wouldn't catch up with me and put her in danger?

I've always known she deserves the world, and I was the idiot who thought I could give it to her. Hell, I couldn't even keep her engagement ring safe! How in the fuck could I be trusted to make sure she's never harmed or put in danger?

The answer is: I can't. I couldn't protect Abigail, and now

Annabelle is about to be dragged into my mess, which is why I haven't called her since I've been on my manhunt for Stan.

After a few hours on the rocks, I got back on my bike and headed for the old neighborhood. Uncle Stew's place isn't far from the apartment where I grew up, and I figured I could welcome Stan home from a long night of fights.

Except he never showed up. And when I pounded on Uncle Stew's door demanding to know where his lowlife piece-of-shit brother was, I was greeted by a hung-over uncle who said he hadn't seen Stan in a few weeks.

The only reason I believed him was because I had him pinned against the wall—nearly cutting off his air supply—before asking him again, only to have him tell me the same thing.

But he did request that if I do find Stan, that I ask for the five hundred bucks he owes him.

Join the club, Uncle Stew.

I spent the rest of that day and the next going to every place I could think of—old bars he used to frequent, where I used to fight, hell, I even swung by my mom's place to make sure he hadn't hit her up for anything.

Each night, though, I ended up back at The Pit well after hours, so no one would see me. If the fights were still going on, I was ready to call the cops on him. Even though it would have ended my business, I would have done it.

Instead I sat in my office, waiting for nothing. No fights. Not a sound all night until I snuck out early each morning. It at least gave me a place to shut my eyes for a few hours so I didn't have to go home and face Annabelle.

I might have been able to avoid her in person, but she haunted my dreams every night. Her sweet smile. Her red hair that I'll still be able to pick out of a crowd when I'm 90. The way her fingers caress the back of my neck when she wraps her arms around me. Her giggle when I kiss places on her that are ticklish.

I hate myself for what I'm doing to her. I know she has to be a mess. But she needs to hate me. Because if she hates me, then she won't want to be near me. And being far away from me is the best thing I can do for her right now.

The same could be said for Stan. But I'm here, and I'm going to end this shit once and for all.

I'm not a small guy, so as I purposefully walk toward the bar, the movement catches Stan's eye. His face goes white when he sees murder in my eyes.

He knows I know. It's all crashing down on him.

"Outside. Now." Not trusting that he'll actually come out, I wait for him to put down his beer, and I walk with him around back. I'm not about to cause a scene in an unfamiliar bar in front of guys I don't know or trust. Plus I need to make sure Stan hears me loud and clear.

"Missed work the past few days. Was getting worried about you."

My statement catches him off-guard. Which is exactly why I said it.

"Yeah. Sorry. I had some business to take care of. Hope I didn't put you out."

I grab him by the shirt and slam him against the building, which he wasn't expecting. I have my elbow against his throat, giving him just enough air to keep him alive.

"You put me out all right. You put me out when you started stealing money from me. You really fucking put me out when I realized Annabelle's engagement ring was missing. And you seriously fucking put me out when two goons showed up looking for you and the money you owe them."

Even after I found out about the illegal fights all those years ago, and then Abigail's death, I never laid a hand on Stan. He wasn't worth it. This confrontation right here is nearly 20 years in the making.

"And then, just when I thought you couldn't fuck with me anymore, I noticed that my gym was being used for some extracurricular events at night. So, Stan, what do you want to admit to first? Because you're going to tell me everything. You're going to give me back my money and Annabelle's ring. And then you're going to have the choice of leaving forever or having me end your pathetic life."

I won't really kill him. I might be a lot of things, but I'm not a murderer. But I need him to know how serious I am. And given that he hasn't taken a real breath in a few minutes, and I'm pretty sure he just pissed himself, I think he gets the picture.

I let him down from against the wall and stand over him. I'll wait all day. He looks up at me like a scared child.

"I swear, when I got out, I wasn't back in it."

But since he can't stop tugging at his earlobe, I know that's a fucking lie. But I don't tell him that. He can't know I know his tells. But at this point, I need to at least try to get some answers.

"Are you running the fights out of the gym?"

He nods.

"Are the cops on to you yet?"

He shrugs. "I think so. That's why we've stayed quiet this week. Needed to get the heat off me."

I bark out a laugh. "Ha! Keep the heat off you? Is the building in your name? Does the bank now all of a sudden have *Stan Kelly* written on the deed? No, you asshole! It's my fucking gym! My gym that you've now made into a fucking fight club. I'll be the one in jail. Not you. But you don't give a shit. You never have."

I can't even look at him right now. But I have more questions. I need more answers. Even if only half of them will be truthful.

"How much money have you stolen from me?"

He sighs. "I'd say around five grand."

"Where is Annabelle's ring?"

He looks at me with remorse in his eyes. This might be the only truthful answer I'll get today. Say what you want to about Stan, but he really did take a liking to my girl.

"I took it to a pawn shop in the old neighborhood."

I want to punch this man. I want to pummel him to the point he's barely breathing.

"What do I need to do to get my money and the damn ring back, my gym cleared out, and you away from me forever?"

Even if Stan leaves town right now, I'm guessing the goons he works with have figured out how to access The Pit. Even if he leaves, what he's created won't go away.

But I need to make it go away. For good.

He pauses, putting both hands in his pockets. Then he says the words I wasn't expecting to hear.

"You. In the ring. One more time."

41

ANNABELLE

I know it's not safe, and that Jaxson would throw a fit if he saw me walking the streets alone at night, but I really don't care right now. If he still wanted a say regarding me or my safety, he shouldn't have just up and left with no word.

Since he's been gone, I go back and forth between wanting to leave the loft and all the memories I've made here, and wanting to never leave this place, thinking that at any moment he could walk through the door and all of this would be over. That we could go back to the way things were just a few days ago.

I can't take how empty the space feels without him—a reminder of how I feel inside since he's been gone. Empty.

Tonight is one of those nights, so when I locked up at the gallery after another paint-and-sip, I just couldn't go home. I needed some space, so now I'm just walking with no destination in mind.

It's been five days now, and with every day that passes, I believe just a little bit more that he's gone for good. In my heart, I know something horrible had to have happened for him to disappear like that. But that doesn't excuse the fact that he just left without a word. Every time I think about that, I just get angrier. I'm at the point where the next time I see him, I don't know if I'll kiss him or slap him. Probably both.

I look up and realize I've somehow ended up at The Pit. Between my work schedule and Jaxson being gone, it feels like forever since I've been here. It's after 11 p.m., and it's been closed for hours, but I notice a light glowing inside. It's faint, but it's there.

I don't know if it's hope or curiosity fueling me, but I head toward the entrance. The glass of the door is frosted, so I can't see anything inside except the slight glow. I grab the doorknob as I bring my body closer to try to hear something, and I'm surprised to find that it easily turns in my hand.

I realize that I should absolutely run away. None of the employees would have left it open. I know I should leave, but that hope-and-curiosity mix propels me toward the light—and toward Jaxson's office.

When I turn the corner, I can hardly believe my eyes. And from the look on his face, Jaxson can hardly believe his either.

I'm speechless. I have so much to say to him, yet I can't find my voice. We stare at each other for what feels like minutes.

Was he here the whole time?

How could he still be within miles of me and not let me know he was okay?

"Why are you here?" he finally asks.

I suck in a breath, bracing myself for what's about to come. "I was walking home from the gallery and saw the light on. I was curious, and the door was unlocked."

"Why were you walking alone at night? God, Annabelle! We've been over this!"

"No!" I scream, cutting him off as I walk into his office. "No! You don't get to care. You don't get to tell me that I'm not being safe! You left me without a word! *Without a word*, Jaxson! Do you know how scared I've been? The thoughts racing through my mind? How worried Kalum and Maverick have been? So, no, you don't get to lecture me after what you've put us through this past week."

I can't seem to catch my breath after unleashing my words on Jaxson.

"You're right," he says, barely above a whisper. "I don't have a right. You're not mine anymore."

My eyes widen and I can't wrap my head around the words he just said.

Did he just say that I'm not his anymore? No. I must have misheard him.

Yes, he'd left me without a word. Yes, I want to strangle him for worrying me. But I never thought that this was it. I'd hoped—no, I knew—that if and when I found him, he would explain everything to me, I would yell at him for scaring me, but in the end, I'd be back in his arms. Where everything was right.

"What did you just say?" I need to make sure I just heard him correctly.

He gets up and walks around the desk, now just inches from me. He goes to reach for my waist out of habit, but quickly puts his hands in his pockets.

I hate this. Even when we were both too scared to admit our feelings for each other, it was never this uncomfortable. This unsure.

"I said I don't have the right. You need to forget about me, Annabelle. I'm not the man for you."

I shake my head, refusing to believe the words he's saying.

"I don't know what you're talking about. Where have you been? Where did you go? Are you in trouble? How can I help? Please, Jaxson, let me in."

I know I'm rambling, but I have to say these things.

"I can't tell you. And you need to leave, Annabelle. You can have the loft. It's yours. Just don't follow me. Don't try to find me. Pretend I never existed."

My tears are flowing in a mix of anger and confusion. I hate him right now. I love him so much, but I hate him. He can't do this to us. I won't let him.

"I don't want to be there if you aren't. You need to come back with me. Let's talk. You can tell me as much or as little as you want to. Just please, Jaxson, *please* come home with me."

I realize I'm begging now, but I don't care. I feel him slipping away from me. The man looking at me now isn't the one who held me in his arms and told me he loved me. This isn't the man who sat and talked with my dad for hours while looking at my baby pictures. This isn't the man I fell in love with.

This isn't even the man who ignored me for months at the café.

I don't know this man. This cold, heartless man might have Jaxson's eyes and body, but this isn't the man I love.

"Then sell it. I don't give a shit. Do whatever you want," he says.

His eyes, usually so expressive, are empty. I don't know what to think anymore. But I feel that the end is near—that I'm only going to have a couple more chances to ask my questions before he kicks me out of his life for good.

"Why did you leave?"

"You don't need to know."

"Are you in trouble?"

He doesn't answer. He just looks at the ground, refusing to make eye contact with me.

"Do you still love me?"

He's silent, refusing to meet my eyes.

I snap.

"Did you ever love me, or was this just some big game to you? Take the shy girl's virginity and make her believe that she found love before getting bored with her?"

Before I know it, he grabs the back of my head and pulls me in, kissing me so hard that I'm sure I'll have bruises in minutes. I don't want to kiss him back, but my body doesn't know how *not* to.

Before we can get too lost in the kiss, he pushes me away, leaving me breathless.

"This was never real. This was both of us thinking we could be people we weren't. That kiss? That was it. Pretend time is over and it's time to go back to the real fucking world where you are an art teacher and I'm a fighter. This is the last time you'll ever see me. I was never good enough for you. I pretended I was. Pretty soon, you would have been bored with me. I'm just ending this before we fool ourselves into thinking we could be more. I'm not the guy who can do forever. So leave. Now."

His words slice through me and I fall to the ground in his office, tears coming so fast I don't even try to stop them.

"You don't mean that. I don't believe you. Whatever you need, we can figure it out. Don't do this to us, Jaxson. Please . . ."

He stands over me, looking down like we were never anything to each other. Like I'm a piece of dirt on his shoe.

"Get up. Leave. Don't look back."

I scramble to my feet and rush out of The Pit, listening to his words. Because if I look back, I'll make a bigger fool of myself. Because I wouldn't just look back. I'd run back. And then I'd once again ask him to give us another chance. To let me help him get past whatever this is all about.

But I know it's useless.

If that's who Jaxson is, then I never knew him at all.

42

JAXSON

I'm glad she listened to me and didn't look back, because if she had, she would have seen tears flowing from my eyes as she ran out of my life.

Like I told her to. Because she can't be around what's about to go down.

Saying those words to her, telling her to leave and forget about us, was the hardest thing I've ever done. But I made sure I didn't say anything about not loving her—because I couldn't lie to her, or myself, about that. But I'll make her think it, because that's what will keep her safe.

I'll love Annabelle Locke until the day I die.

Which could be tomorrow if this fight goes wrong.

I can't believe she walked in here. I'd only unlocked the front door so Kalum and Maverick could get in. I'd texted Kalum right before Annabelle barged in, though he's probably going to be more pissed than she was.

I don't blame them. I disappeared while on my mission to once and for all get my father out of my life. Only I never expected that this is what I'd have to go through to make that happen.

A few minutes after Annabelle leaves, the two men who have

known me the longest walk into my gym, looking like they're out for blood. My blood.

"Where the fuck have you been?" Kalum screams, his strides purposeful as he closes the distance between us then punches me square in the jaw.

"What the fuck, man?" I say as I try to move my jaw, hoping he didn't break it.

"That's for ghosting us." He then kicks me in the stomach. "And that's for us finding Annabelle waiting for a cab, sobbing outside your fucking gym. What the fuck, man? It's one thing to go silent on us, but Annabelle doesn't deserve that."

I sit up, trying to get the wind back in me.

"I broke it off with her. I can't bring her into this shit, so I told her to leave. She's gone."

I crawl up to one of the benches by the boxing ring, trying to shake out the pain in my jaw.

"Jaxson, seriously man, where have you been? We looked everywhere. Where did you go? What is going on?" This time, Maverick asks. As always, he gets to be the good cop.

"I had shit to take care of."

"Shit you couldn't tell us about?" Kalum says. "We have always told each other everything, especially when shit got bad. Everything! So fuck you for worrying us. And fuck you for leaving your girl worried sick. You were right all those months ago. You don't deserve her."

I slump over, knowing that everything Kalum is saying is true. I have been a bastard. I'm a grade-A asshole.

And I don't deserve love from someone like Annabelle.

"I didn't want anyone getting dragged into this. It was my mess. And I needed to clean it up."

"And have you?" Maverick asks. "Is that why you've all of a sudden decided to deem us worthy of knowing what's going on with you?"

I shake my head. "No. But I do know I need your help."

"I'm not helping you until I know what the fuck is going on," Kalum says, still clearly angry at me. "You don't get to all of a sudden come back and expect us to just go along with whatever the fuck you've been up to."

I straighten myself, bracing for the backlash.

"Stan is in deep. He's been stealing money from me and stole the engagement ring I had for Annabelle."

"That fucker!" Kalum yells. "Did you find him? Did you pound his face in? Please tell me you have now officially written off that asshole."

I suck in a breath, preparing for the worst.

"It took me a few days, but I finally tracked him down. He's $200,000 in the hole. And he's been using the gym at night to run fights."

Kalum and Maverick just stare at me, making sure the words I just said were real.

"When did you find out?" Maverick is the first to speak.

"The night before I took off."

"Do the cops know?" Kalum asks, knowing as well as anyone that I can't have the cops breathing down my neck if I want to avoid another trip to prison.

"Not that I know of."

I tell them about how I found out about the fights, and the debt, and what I have to do to make all this go away. That I have to get in a ring again.

"He wants you to fucking fight? You can't," Kalum quickly says.

"I agree," Mav chimes in. "Do you think this is actually going to work out? How can you trust anything he says at this point?"

I agree with both of them. I might still spar at the gym, but I am in no way fight-ready. And I'd bet all the money that Stan hasn't stolen from me that the fight will somehow be fixed.

"I know. I don't want to, but right now it's the only way I can make this stop and get Stan out of my life. So it looks like I have to."

We sit quietly for a minute, processing everything. How did my life come to this? Wasn't it just a few weeks ago that I was trying to figure out how I wanted to propose to Annabelle? That I thought I was actually getting to a better place with Stan?

I might have thrown words at Annabelle to make her hate me, but there is one thing I said that was the truth—I was never good enough for her. And the fact that I have to get back in the ring to pay off a debt that's not mine—maybe with my life—is proof enough.

"I need you guys there. I need you in my corner. I don't know how this is going to go down, but I need as many friendly faces as I can get so I don't die in that ring."

Maverick sits down next to me, slapping his hand over my knee. "We're there. You don't even have to ask."

I look up at Kalum, my oldest friend. The one I'd walk through fire for. I see the debate in his eyes. He hates this as much as I do.

"Kalum? You with me?"

He sighs, running a hand through his hair.

"I'm there. We'll do what we need to do. Just like we always have."

ANNABELLE

"Are you sure this is a good idea?" Tori asks me, gripping the passenger door of my car as we race across town to Maverick and Kalum's shop.

"No, but I don't have a better one and I need backup."

I didn't go back to the loft last night. I couldn't. It hurt too much to even think about going back there. Not after what he said to me and how I was practically begging him not to end this. Not to end *us*.

I was embarrassed when Kalum and Maverick found me outside The Pit. I didn't speak to them; I just cried into Kalum's shoulder until Maverick got an Uber to take me to Tori's, where I stayed last night.

But after my tears stopped, which was many hours later, I realized that the only reason those two would have been together, outside The Pit at that time of night, was if they knew Jaxson was there.

Which means they know more than they're telling me.

"What if they know just as much as we do?" Tori asks gently.

"Then I can at least know that I tried. I know he's keeping things from me. I don't know if it's just about his dad, or if it's more, but I have to try, Tori. It can't end like this. It just can't."

The worst part is that I don't know if what he said last night was the truth, or just a truth in his mind. He's told me many times that he doesn't deserve me. That he isn't good enough for me. And I've tried everything I can do to make him realize he's exactly what I need.

But saying it was pretend? That it was never real? That's what stung. And although I still believe he was throwing daggers to hurt me on purpose, part of me wonders if it was true—if I was so blinded by my infatuation with him that it clouded reality.

Kalum and Maverick are my last hope.

We pull up to their shop and luckily, it's not busy. We find them in the garage, both looking inside the hood of some sort of classic car.

I don't want to scare them, so I approach slowly. But apparently Tori doesn't care. She strides right over, all while taking a glance at Kalum bending over the car.

"Don't stare at the goods if you don't intend on buying anything," Kalum says, scaring Tori out of her daydream.

"I don't know what you're talking about," she says hurriedly, clearly trying to play off the fact that he just caught her red-handed.

These two really just need to get together and get it over with.

The brothers stand up from the car, looking at me with sadness in their eyes.

"How are you holding up, Annabelle?" Maverick asks.

"I'm confused. And angry. So angry. But hurt and sad and I just want answers."

The two of them look at each other, saying things with their eyes that only a sibling could decode.

"We don't have the answers you need," Kalum says.

I figured this would be their response. But I'm not giving up that easily.

"Then why were you two at The Pit last night?"

"Why were you?" Maverick asks, feeling me out.

"I was walking, trying to clear my head, and my feet just took me there. I saw the light on and the door was unlocked."

The brothers look at each other and Kalum nods at Maverick. "Jaxson texted us. Asked us to meet him down there."

"What did he want? What did he say? Please, tell me *something*." I know I'm begging again, but this is what desperation sounds like.

"That, we can't tell you. I'm sorry, Annabelle. I really am."

"No, you are fucking not!" Tori snaps at Maverick. "You aren't sorry. You're covering for your friend, which I get. He's basically your brother. But you're *our* friends now too, and this girl is hurting because the man who supposedly loves her is keeping things from her and breaking her heart. So, no, you don't get to be fucking sorry."

Kalum gets in her face. "Do you think we like keeping these secrets? Do you think we like that he took off on us too? No! I fucking decked him last night when I walked into the gym because the man is pissing me off too. But he's my brother. And he asked for help. I'm going to give him that because that's how we can keep him alive."

His words startle me and as soon as they leave his mouth. He quickly realizes he's said too much.

"What do you mean 'keep him alive'? What's going on, Kalum? Please, I have to know."

He takes a deep breath before turning to me. "I'm only telling you this because I'm an idiot and ran my mouth. Jaxson would kill me if he found out you knew. So here goes: his dad is in pretty deep with gambling debts, so he started running illegal fights out of The Pit. Jaxson found out. But now, Stan's blackmailing him. The only way for this to go away is for Jaxson to fight."

I'm speechless. Stunned. I can't wrap my head around this.

"When?" I need to know.

"Tonight."

The tears spring from my eyes and I drop to the floor—Tori quickly coming to my side to comfort me. There's been too much thrown at me over the past week. I can't process it all.

"You *have* to stop him." I look up, pleading with his two best friends.

"We tried. He dug his heels in," Maverick says. "But we all realize this fight won't be on the level. So we're going to be in his corner. Try to figure out what the fix is so we can make sure he doesn't end up dead."

No. He can't do this. He can't fight. He can't die. He just . . . can't.

"I want to go with you."

Tori, Kalum, and Maverick all look at me like I'm crazy.

"No. Not even a chance, Annabelle," Kalum says, pacing around the shop in exasperation. "Jaxson's already going to kill me for telling you. There is *no* way you're going to that fight."

Maverick chimes in. "I agree. The lowlifes who will be there aren't to be messed with. These are the kind of men who killed an innocent teenager because her dad fucked them over. It's too dangerous. You need to stay away."

Poor Maverick. The sadness that takes over his face when talking about Abigail is heartbreaking. I hate that he, Kalum, and Jaxson had to go through that so young.

Tori squeezes me a little harder, trying to be the last voice of reason. "Jaxson needs to keep his head on straight. If he realizes you're there, you could do more harm than good. If he's going to do this, he needs to stay focused. And you being there is a surefire way for his head to not be in the game."

I nod. I know they're right.

But I also know that nothing could stop me from going.

44

JAXSON

I was never a superstitious boxer. I had a routine, but I never thought that if I didn't do something, I would lose a fight.

But as I stare at my taped-up hands, prepping for a fight I don't want to be in but have to be part of, I know something is missing. So I grab a Sharpie, rip off the cap with my teeth, then write the initials "A.L." on the top of my left hand.

I'm doing this for her. I might have had to hurt her in the process, but this is how I'll keep her safe. Because if everything goes the way it's supposed to tonight, I know she'll be unharmed.

"You ready?" Stan comes into my office as I'm loosening up.

Yes, part of the deal I had to make was allowing one more fight at The Pit. We closed early for a "private function."

I hate this. I hate everything about it. But I've gone over it a hundred times and I don't see another way out. Because the men Stan owes money to don't care about my business, or the people I love. They just want their money. And until they have it back, they will make my life a living hell.

"As ready as I'll ever be." I stand up, trying to shake out the tension in my arms.

"Thanks for doing this, Son. I can't tell you how much—"

"Stop," I cut him off, anger pouring through my words. "Don't call me *son*. You have lost the right to call me that. Tonight is the last time you'll ever see me. I'm not doing this for you. I'm doing this for you to get the hell out of my life."

He drops his head. "I know. I'm sorry I got us in this mess."

"No, you aren't. You're sorry you didn't win."

He doesn't reply. He turns to grab my gloves and help me slip them on. Normally, this is something that Kalum would do, but I've sent the brothers on a much more important mission. The most important one of the night.

"Do we need to go over again how this is going to go down?"

We don't, but I'm not going to tell him that. He's fixed the fight, and at least this time he's letting me in on the secret.

"Sure."

He rubs his earlobe before explaining, which is all the sign I need to know that what I'm about to do is the right move.

"The kid you're fighting hasn't lost yet, so having you as a challenger has brought in some big bets. But everyone is going with you. I swear, kid, even years later you still bring the big coin."

He says it like he's a proud dad and I just won a medal at the science fair.

"The betting is all on you knocking him out in the eighth round. But I need you to do it in the sixth."

My head snaps up. That's not how it was supposed to go.

"Why the sixth? Does Dominic know?"

Dominic is the kid I'm fighting. I've actually met him a few times when he's come in to spar with a buddy of his. Good fighter. But he's not exactly the type to take a fall.

Good thing he won't be.

"No, he doesn't. He thinks it's on the level. So I'm going to need you to make sure you throw something he doesn't get up from. But I should let you know, it will be very beneficial for the both of us if you do it in the sixth."

Stan finishes taping up my gloves and walks away as Kalum walks in, staring at Stan like he wants to murder him on the spot.

"You ready?" he asks, making sure my gloves are on tight.

"As ready as I'm ever going to be."

I then ask the most important question of the night.

"Is Dominic ready?"

For the first time in a few days, my best friend gives me a smile.

"Yes, he's happy to help."

———

THE BELL SOUNDS to end the fourth round. While I've been holding up pretty well, my body definitely knows that it's been a while since I've done this.

Which makes me even more glad it's almost over.

I head back to my corner, where Kalum and Maverick are waiting to tend to me. Dominic got in a few punches that round, which will make this round even more believable.

This will be the first round, and first fight, I'll ever lose in my life.

"You ready to do this?" Maverick asks, wiping some blood away from my eyes.

"Never been so sure about anything. This ends. Now."

Kalum sprays some water in my mouth, which I swish around and spit into the bucket before standing back up. I catch Stan's eye as he's leaning against a back wall with a smug smile on his face.

Fuck him. Fuck him for putting me in this position. He's about to get everything he deserves.

I meet Dominic back in the center of the ring, and we touch gloves for the next round to begin. The kid is good, I'll admit that. I would have loved to have fought him in a straight fight back in my younger days.

I connect with a few jabs, which purposely leave my midsection open as he gets me with a few punches to the stomach. I keel over a bit—the blows knocking the wind out of me. I stumble back to the ropes and he comes at me again, but I block him, so we're clinched together, looking like we're in a bro hug.

"Now. I need you to do it now," I say to him.

He knows what I am asking him to do, though it wasn't supposed to be this early. But after Stan said he needed me to knock him out in the sixth, I had to call an audible. I just didn't have time to tell Dominic before the fight started.

"You sure?" he asks, still trying to land small punches to make this look believable.

"Yes. Now."

It's all I have to say as I find a second wind and push us off the ropes. I try throwing a series of punches, but only a few land.

I leave myself open and he comes at me with a left hook that makes me see stars. My legs buckle and I'm down.

I've lost the fight, but I've won so much more.

All I hear are screams and boos from the crowd—degenerates pissed because I lost them a shit-ton of money.

I peel myself from the canvas and see the guys Stan is in deep with. They nod at me and I nod back. This simple gesture lets me know we're square—that I just got my gym back.

That was Maverick's job before the fight. I knew that Stan had rigged it for me to win, but I needed to make sure that not only did I lose, but that I got free from the guys he was in with. Because they were the ones who posed the real danger.

Luckily, I realized they only cared about the money. So we found the two guys who so graciously visited me at the gym, and we set up how we were going to flip the rig. With everyone betting on me, the payout for Dominic winning was huge, especially before the eighth round. They put a shitload of money on Dominic.

They won back the money Stan owed them, plus a few thousand extra. And in turn, for me throwing the fight, they promised to never come near my gym again. And they gave their word that they'd leave me and my loved ones alone.

While I'm relieved that a part of this is over, another part of me needs to see Stan. I need to see his face.

I stand up, looking around for the man I will never again call my father. I need to see the look in his eyes as he realizes I just got my gym back, and him out of my life, while fucking him over in the process.

But all I see is a blaze of red hair leaving through the back door. Red hair that I would know anywhere.

45

ANNABELLE

I knew I shouldn't have gone to the fight. But I couldn't stay away.

Seeing Jaxson in that ring was like nothing I could have imagined. I had watched him spar many times. We used to work out together and I'd admire the way his arms and body reacted when he was hitting the heavy bag.

But seeing him up there tonight, the way he moved around that ring, so focused, was the sexiest thing I had ever witnessed.

I hightailed it back to the loft as soon as it was over, wanting to make sure no one saw me. I just needed to feel close to him. I put on one of his T-shirts and sat on the couch, thinking of all the nights we sat in this same spot, him holding me while we talked about everything and nothing.

All I can think about is Jaxson in that ring. I hated seeing him in there, putting himself in that kind of danger because of Stan.

But I can't lie; it also totally turned me on.

I stayed in the back, away from the action, but I could see everything.

His muscles rippling when he threw punches at his opponent.

His eyes when they were locked in. I've missed those eyes looking at me. So determined. So sexy.

And I saw his face when he went down. At first I was shocked, and I gasped when he fell to the mat. He didn't lose. He never lost.

Then I saw his face when he got up, and I knew.

He threw the fight.

I don't know why, but I have to believe he knew what he was doing. And hopefully, that brings him back to me.

———

I DON'T KNOW when I fell asleep, but I wake up on the couch to find a blanket over me.

Except I didn't have a blanket when I nodded off last night.

I open my eyes and see Jaxson sitting by my feet, with a hand on my leg and my favorite brown eyes looking at me like he's never seen me before.

"When did you come in?" I ask.

"Probably about 4 a.m. You were asleep. I didn't want to wake you," he says quietly, gently caressing my leg.

"Why did you come to the fight?"

I sit up, not knowing how this is going to go, and needing to brace myself for anything.

"I needed to see for myself that you were okay."

He sighs before pinching the bridge of his nose. He's showered since last night, but his eyes look tired. Not just from the night, but probably from the past week finally catching up with him.

"I'm fine. It's all over." He lets out a breath I'm pretty sure he's been holding since this whole ordeal started.

"Is your dad gone?"

If he's surprised that I ask about Stan, he doesn't show it. "Yeah. For good this time. I'm so sorry I brought him into our lives. I was so stupid to think—"

I move closer, tenderly placing a finger to his lips, silencing him.

"You were not stupid. You were a man with a heart who gave someone a second chance. Stan is the stupid one who ruined his chance of ever knowing how great his son is. I can't believe he took advantage of you like that. I'm sorry for pushing you to let him in."

He takes my finger from his mouth and links his fingers through mine. Just holding his hand like this, feeling his touch, is giving me hope that we're going to be okay. But until I hear the words, I refuse to get my hopes up too high.

"It's not your fault. You're right. It was his. But he's gone now. Out of our lives forever. Tonight, during the fight, I took the fall. I hated it. I never wanted to knowingly fix a fight. But it was what I had to do to make sure Stan was gone and the gym would be left alone. And that you . . . that they . . ."

I put my arms around him as he fights back his emotions. It's then that I realize how much this was bringing up the past for him—that he was trying to protect me the way he couldn't protect his sister.

"I'm fine. Everyone is okay. It's over, Jaxson. It's over."

We sit like that for I don't know how long. I'm pretty sure he's fallen asleep until his words startle me.

"I'm sorry for everything I said. I needed you to stay away. I needed you safe. And the only way I knew how to do that was for you to be as far away from me as possible. I said words to make you hate me. I'm so sorry, Annabelle. I'm so fucking sorry."

"I know," I say as I rub the back of his neck. "I know you thought you were doing the right thing. But Jaxson, I've never been so scared as when you left. Not even the night I was attacked. But not knowing where you were, or if you were alive . . . I can never go through that again."

He sits up and pulls me into his lap.

"I'm so sorry. I know it was stupid, but I was in a rage."

"You told me you'd never disappear on me like that. That when it got hard, you'd talk to me. Not only did you not tell me where you were, but then when I did find you, the words you said hurt me deeply. I don't know which way is up right now. Sitting here like this makes me think that we're going to be okay. But what happens when it gets hard again? I can't live my life wondering if today's going to be the day you leave me again."

He wipes a tear that's escaped my eye and gently presses his lips to mine. This kiss is so different from our last one in his office. Where that kiss filled me with dread and finality, this kiss gives me hope.

"I will apologize to you for what I did for the rest of our lives. And I promise, from now on, I will never keep anything like that from you ever again."

He takes a deep breath and brings me closer to him.

"You are my life, Annabelle. What I fought for tonight wasn't just the gym, or just to get Stan out of my life. It was for you. For your safety, so I could love you again the way you deserve. I love you so much it hurts. This last week has been torture without you. And I promise, from this day forward, I will always talk to you. You're my lover. My partner. My best friend. I can't spend another day without you. And I hope, even though I don't deserve one, that you will give me another chance to love you."

My tears are flowing, but I don't care. He's back. My Jaxson is back.

I cup his face and bring my lips to his, pouring my love, forgiveness, and soul into it. He returns the favor, deepening the kiss. Our tongues find each other and I know that we could kiss like this all night.

Slowly, we separate our lips and just look at each other. Two people who couldn't be more different now knowing that we're nothing if we aren't together.

"I love you, Annabelle Locke. Do you forgive me? Will you let me have another chance?"

I kiss him one more time, simply because I can.

"I will. Under one condition."

He tucks a loose strand of hair behind my ear. "Anything."

"Never throw a fight again. I don't associate with losers."

Before I know it, Jaxson is lifting me up and tossing me over his shoulder as we make our way to the bedroom.

"You want a winner? I'll show you how we can both be winners."

And he does. Multiple times.

EPILOGUE

JAXSON

I remember how I thought I was nervous when Annabelle and I first got together.

And then when I met her father.

Or when I thought I had lost her for good.

But those were all child's play compared to the nerves I'm feeling today.

It's been three months since my final fight, when I almost lost it all only to get back more than I'd ever dreamed of.

Since then, things have been perfect. Annabelle's classes are taking off, and they're so full she has to turn kids away, which she hates. The gym's membership is at an all-time high and I've been approached about holding semi-annual fight nights. The legal kind where amateur fighters can cut their teeth.

And I couldn't be happier knowing that every night I get to come home to Annabelle.

I'm one lucky son of a bitch. I hate a lot of parts about my past. I miss my sister every day. But it's led me here, and for that, I'm grateful.

"You ready?" Tori asks me from behind the counter at Perks.

"I am." I might be nervous, but I'm as sure as ever that I want Annabelle to be with me for the rest of my life.

When Tori sees her coming around the corner, she signals for me to hide in the back. Luckily, it's not far from the counter, so I can hear their conversation, and there's a little window I can look through so I'll know when it's time for me to surprise her.

"Hey girl!" Tori says, probably a little too loudly.

"Hi! What was the big emergency you needed me down here for? I'm supposed to meet Jaxson at the loft soon."

If she knows what's coming, she doesn't let on. I tried to act normal this morning before she went to work, and I was hoping I was a better actor than I felt I was.

"Do I need a reason to see my best friend? That hurts, Annabelle. That hurts deep."

Annabelle rolls her eyes. "No, you don't need an excuse. But you could have asked me over for a girls' night instead of coming here."

"I could have, but I needed to give you back your sweater. I'll run to the back and get it. Do you want a latte before I grab it?"

"You know I can't say no to one. Make it strong and go get me my sweater that I apparently need to have back."

I watch Tori from the window, making the latte. She takes the cup, ensuring the correct side is facing Annabelle when she hands it over.

"Give me a few. I'll be right back."

Tori comes through the door, a smile from ear to ear.

"You're up."

I take the deepest breath of my life and exit the door, coming around to her side of the counter. Just like I'd hoped, by the time I'm in front of her, she's already reading what's written on the cup.

Annabelle, will you marry me?

I hear her gasp as she turns toward me and I get down on one knee.

"Jaxson! What . . . are you . . . ?"

Tears are starting to well in her eyes and if I don't say what I need to, mine will soon follow.

"Annabelle, from the first time I saw you in this coffee shop, I knew there was something different about you. I tried to stay away, but I couldn't. And even when I tried to push you away, you wouldn't let me. You fought for us through everything, and I thank my lucky stars that you're the real fighter in this relationship."

Her hand is covering her mouth, trying to contain her sobs.

"Annabelle, will you marry me? I promise you, from this day forward, and for the rest of our lives, we will fight together. We will make it through what life throws at us, because you make me stronger. You make me a better man. I love you, Annabelle. Marry me?"

I open the box to show her the engagement ring I thought I'd never see again. As soon as Stan told me where he tried to pawn it, I rushed to the shop, praying it was still there. Because it wasn't an eye-popping ring, no one had bought it. I purchased it back for probably more than the guy ever thought he'd get, but it was worth twice that to see the look on Annabelle's face right now.

"Is that my mom's?"

I nod. "Yes. Your dad gave it to me. He said she wanted you to have it."

She's a complete mess now, but she's never looked more beautiful. And although I'm pretty sure she thinks she's said *yes*, I haven't heard the words, and that is kind of fucking with me right now.

"Tell him 'yes,' Annabelle! Don't make the poor guy wait!" Tori yells from the back.

Annabelle chuckles between her sobs. "Yes, Jaxson. A thousand times yes. I will marry you."

I place the ring on her finger and scoop her up to me, needing to kiss the woman I'm going to get to call my wife.

"I love you, Annabelle. So much. Thank you for fighting for me."

"I love you, Jaxson Kelly. Thank you for saving me."

READ THE REST OF THE SOUTH SIDE BOYS SERIES

Broken-Book 2
Wrecked-Book 3
Redemption-Book 4 (Coming February)

ALSO BY ALEXIS WINTER

Hate That I Love You: Castille Hotel Series Prequel

Want this prequel for FREE? Sign up here to get it along with a second free novel delivered right to your inbox!

Castille Hotel Series

Business & Pleasure: Castille Hotel Series Book 1

Baby Mistake: Castille Hotel Series Book 2

Fake It: Castille Hotel Series Book 3

Make Her Mine Series

My Best Friend's Brother

Billionaire With Benefits

My Boss's Sister

My Best Friend's Ex

The Friend Agreement (Coming this March)

Mountain Ridge Series

Just Friends: Mountain Ridge Book 1

Protect Me: Mountain Ridge Book 2

Baby Shock: Mountain Ridge Book 3

Claimed by Him: A Contemporary Romance 6 Book Collection

ALL BOOKS CAN BE READ AS STAND-ALONE READS WITHIN THESE SERIES

ABOUT THE AUTHOR

Alexis Winter is a contemporary romance author who loves to share her steamy stories with the world. She specializes in billionaires, alpha males and the women they love.

If you love to curl up with a good romance book you will certainly enjoy her work. Whether it's a story about an innocent young woman learning about the world or a sassy and fierce heroin who knows what she wants you,'re sure to enjoy the happily ever afters she provides.

When Alexis isn't writing away furiously, you can find her exploring the Rocky Mountains, traveling, enjoying a glass of wine or petting a cat.

You can find her books on Amazon or at
https://www.alexiswinterauthor.com/

Follow Alexis Winter below for access to advanced copies of upcoming releases, fun giveaways and exclusive deals!

Made in the USA
Coppell, TX
27 July 2020